my ghost in the bush of lies

my ghost in the bush of lies
paul wessels

ISBN: 0-9584542-8-0

deep south
p.o. box 6082
grahamstown
6140
www.deepsouth.co.za
contact@deepsouth.co.za

We gratefully acknowledge financial assistance for publishing this book from
The National Arts Council

deep south titles are distributed by
University of KwaZulu-Natal Press
www.ukznpress.co.za
books@ukzn.ac.za

Cover and text design : Paul Wessels
Layout : Martin Hiller

Thanks are due to Doug and Lyn Wessels, Dreyer Kruger, Robert Berold, Cindy Harris, Aryan Kaganof, Stacy Hardy, Hüsker Dü, Pere Ubu, Vader Jakob, and Not Even The TV.

I am no longer myself but thought's aptitude for finding itself and spreading across a plane that passes through me at several places.

Gilles Deleuze & Félix Guattari

Follow the leader, don't lead the followers.

Paulus Nomad

The only constant about a cloud is its inconsistency.
Constantly inconsistent. Clouds can be eaten as ice-cream,
or drunk as water – the cold mountain streams – or eaten
as mushrooms, fungicidal spores. Clouds are also Black Elk.
Clouds can be diabolical or simply evanescent or better still,
incalculable. In childhood, a cloud holds a shape for as long
as a pictogram holds the attention – which is, that is, until it
no longer does so. In later life, it holds the attention no longer
than it takes for a second, third, fourth, fifth impression to
wrest the eye back to the horizon. Or is that away from the
horizon? Nevertheless, our eye soon returns and returns
again. There is an unambiguous constant returning to the
source of effervescence. As the wind blows the hair into my
face, so my eye is drawn to the clouds. It is ridiculous to
believe in seeing little people, tiny creatures in the clouds.
The stupidity of sitting on a cloud. A cloud is about as close
to the human as a brick is. No. The cloud attracts our eye,
gathers our thoughts, displaces our certainties because so
dissimilar to us, so antithetical to our sensibilities which seek
constancy within inertia, solidity within form. Clouds present
us with the impossibility of stagnancy, the impossibility of
form, the fact of inconsistency, the fact of perpetual motion.
The cloud is also the greatest non-physical mass observable.
A mass without value. This is not Spirit. This is cloud. Does
God originate in the clouds? The cloud is the physical or
visible manifestation of gas. Also the precursor of rain, shade,
terrible destruction, frightening beauty. Like a billowing cloud
is not like a rolling stone. A cloud mediates the blue sky and
the brown earth. Chinese clouds are no different to Alaskan
clouds. One face is just the same as another. I imagine
a little dog looking at a cloud with a cocked head and a
puzzled brow, who, just like a cloud, suffers from ambition
exceeding capacity. Of course, neither a cloud nor a dog
can have ambition. Precisely. I hear the rustle of trees as
much as the straining of motor vehicles beneath the clouds.
An aeroplane! An aeroplane, a small aeroplane, probably
a two-seater, explodes into existence between myself and
the clouds. It is not at all the same as a helicopter. That is

altogether another matter entirely. But an aeroplane! A small
two-seater is like a thread lost between two seams of fabric.
And clouds can differ considerably amongst themselves.
Clouds drag wind in their wake? Why not. They know nothing
of it. And when it seems a light dimmer has been turned
right down? When a cloud occludes the sun, or clouds amass
to bring stormy skies and rain, hail, snow, sleet. And there it
is. A cloud draws me from my reverie and back to itself for
further contemplation. Clouds are like dreams. These massive
volumes of nothingness nonetheless have a profound impact
upon us regardless of our will or feelings on the matter.
Just as that cloud overhead passes by without our notice,
so too can a dream occur without notice. But it did occur.
And recurs. Some clouds lick and whisp upon themselves.
Curl and churn in their brilliant whiteness. Some clouds sit
obdurately on a blue background. Like flocks of birds, clouds
promote dynamic or contradictory cohesion and uniformity.
This radical fluidity is utterly anti-human. Representation
cannot represent itself. We draw alongside enormity only
to be sucked by undertow to oblivion and irrelevance. The
wind insists the clouds depart. The clouds drag wind in their
wake. Ridiculous. Clouds drag yachts, kites, wind. Birds
defy clouds. Birds and clouds are very alike. And are you
ever more aware of clouds as when there are none? Or just
one? The human really is a cur. Why the inclination for the
eyes always to drop earthwards, and not to fall? Upwards?
Perhaps because there we meet our anti-matter. A cloud can
resemble the mud prawn in shape but not essence. Clouds
can also appear out of focus.

#

I don't love him any. Is really, really difficult hurt and I hate
seeing frustrates me. I told can come over at least if possible,
because I much, I need to be time with you what? I March
1989 I will I cannot realise how me, and I do love who really
– it is so strange my first love with you. I have before for any
to me and caring. Good luck with study very hard the same

thing. So let us work one of your I hope to with the name of our you with the happiness that into my life and you my love with the that I have for you. What to so to you what I can say is so much and I all my being. I don't that I fall in love anyway I don't regret you sorry if pressurising you, that I like this me. So my love made mine but it. I love you what? I am I think we need to we do really love each other, we are grown ups to play around with to hurt other people. Decided what to do, for you to make your about the whole situation. Don't deal with this won't be any trust that may lead us to of which I will hate. Up to you to decide, you who know your heart feelings. Therefore stop this I don't like say in my life. I one person, I can't end I don't want to I love with someone – can't stand it. Try to think of what I mean you already want, so perhaps it better to tell me, I where I stand... So accept that, and I will not you will be – it sounds as consider that if other. I mean there is no time each others I have already but will wait final decision I mean if we problem now, between us, and terminate our love however, it is the only one and your this song: Count on Houston and C Winans? Do know this song love it because, I love with all my heart. You know I feel this way for you for me, this is not but to be honest ever felt this way – you are so special are so sweet and your studies end because I am doing this is our last year hard. Please send me please! You soon and favour, drive carefully. It has feeling into my heart feeling is true love, I do love you. I spend more time, with you know you better.

#

I move my tongue around the acrid, cheesy sperm, pushing it against my teeth before swallowing.

Magda looked up at him. He thought she smiled. The dream environment flattened as if it were a gigantic painting, cracking peeling from the canvas, leaving him in darkness.

I lose myself in the words that create me. They make me

*all up because they hate the inside, most of all me. They're
everywhere. I am nowhere.*

A man committing vast tracts of philosophy to memory and a
madman with a knife standing above him claiming a finger of
his own for every mistake.

*I pull my jeans on. Get a shirt. I'm sore from too much sun.
I'm sore from too much fucking.*

He brings coffee to the table.

*I moved in with heroin and despair. The heroin ran out.
Loomer moved in.*

He says: "I've yet to see the minds of my generation,
destroyed or otherwise."

There's a knock on the door. It's Cherry.

"Magda," she says. "Paulus Nomad's been arrested."

*Paulus Nomad's been arrested. I have tears of blood coming
out my bum from being fucked last night. Tears of come
in the condom lying on the floor next to the bed. Tears of
whiskey swallowed by my drunken liver. Tears of sweat on
my white sunburnt back. Seeping cuts from sjamboks in
the night searching out youth. Nicotine tongues searching
through smarmy lyrics to drown out the lies. Paulus Nomad's
been arrested.*

I did not know Paulus Nomad well or claim to understand
him. He invited me out one evening to visit a man he
introduced as Loomer. When we arrived at his apartment,
he was slouched in the doorway, sneering at us. At first I
thought he was looking past us as we approached along

the narrow corridor. He ushered us in, closed the door. The apartment was completely trashed. There was damp running down the walls feeding moss and algae, seeping into an already saturated carpet. Everything had been smashed, mangled, torn, broken. Records lying all over the place. Books ripped to shreds. Cassette tape strewn from the light fittings and attached to the sealed window frames. It was unbelievable. In the centre of the room, amid all this junk was a mattress with two people on it. They were Magda and Cherry. I stripped down and positioned myself somewhere between them. "Fuckit man, can't a crowd get a bit of space here," shrieked Magda (I think). My legs were suddenly hoisted into the air, and my feet slapped the sides of my head as Loomer fucked me soundly. Cherry got off the bed, pulled on a dress – a torn dress – and was speaking on her cell phone: "Sometimes I get to feeling kinda crazy, and sometimes I get to feeling kind of bored..." Nomad sprang from somewhere, tackling her like a fucking rugby player. They went crashing through the junk. Cherry was laughing hysterically, screaming "A dog grunting in the distance. A woman barking in my bed". Then Loomer shot a load of come in my eyes, so I had to busy myself with that. When I was done, Nomad and Cherry had disappeared. I disentangled myself from Loomer and headed for where I thought I'd find the bathroom. Passing a bedroom, I saw Nomad lying on a bed, clutching a deflated blow-up doll, bearing a very disturbing resemblance to Cherry. He looked up at me, his eyes were red, he'd cut his face open, probably from the dive he made in the other room. Sobbing, he kept repeating "I humped and I pumped and I blew her away, man". Just then, Magda walked past us, and stood against the wall. "Young men," she says, "what you're trying to regain through your cocks, I already have in my heart. And what you're trying to express with your fists, I forgave you before you began." She then shits like a fucking rocket, standing straight up, against the wall. Nomad jumps up, the tears and anguish seemingly forgotten for the moment, stands in front of Magda and screams in her face, "Fuck off you old whore. I want whatever fist I can get up my rectum, down my throat, through my fucking skull if that's where I think it best to fit, so fuck the fuck off!" Unperturbed, Magda replies, "Oh the degradation." Nomad then turns to me, says: "Let's weird this pasture for better shitholes yet."

#

November, after his return to Frankfort, he wrote to Hegel: "It is very good that the infernal spirits, which I took with me from Franconia, and the aerial spirits with metaphysical wings which escorted me out of Jena, have left me since I came to Frankfort." The whole thing began with a blunder on my part, an entirely innocent piece of clumsiness, a gaffe, as the French call it. In architecture, pointed arches have been used elsewhere as a means of decoration, in antiquity and in Asia; presumably the combination of pointed arch and cross-arched vault was not unknown in the Orient. It would be hard to find any reputable literary critic today who would care to be caught defending as an idea the old antithesis of style versus content. To this extent, nihilism, as the denial of a truthful world, of being, might be a divine way of thinking. There is a kind of fatal strategy of conformity. Cynthia Citibank was after meat day and night. "We may all be nature's noblemen," he was saying, and the mention of a nobleman made Félix feel happier the instant he caught the word, though what followed left him in some doubt, "but think of the stories that do not amount to much!" Therefore we frequently see those who in life conquered in every battle; when it was a future enemy they had to deal with, they became powerless, their arms paralysed. When Kierkegaard speaks of hiin Enkelte in his dedicatory preface, he means more than we do by our words "that individual." For example, it was he who had

---

* This and all similar lengthy italicised interventions are made up of the first complete sentence on page 15 of some books in my possession at various times of writing.

already replaced Rakoski with Nagy. What did they call such young people in Goethe's Germany? Then enterprising city men themselves took over farms, enlarged the dwelling houses and set up as summer landlords, especially in Sullivan, Ulster, and Greene Counties. At ten o'clock on Tuesday we got a call from the shipping line saying our heavy luggage — two suitcases of clothes and a box of books — had to be on board the Pleasantville by ten-thirty Wednesday morning. Towler had tried to give opium up more than once, and had failed, and now he was hopeless. Note the attack on the Royal Society; and the parallel between the new secular building and the "Fabrick" that "rose like an exhalation" in the opening passage from Milton, which also compares the way Pandaemonium was built to the passage of air into the pipes of an organ. Then a visit to the Canterbury Music Hall, sitting in a red plush seat watching my father perform...

Let's summon the ghost of Paulus Nomad, says Loomer.

Magda: *"I create myself in the words that create me. I make it all up in order that it shall make me up. I cannot stop now."*

Loomer: *"Death be not proud, though some have called thee Mighty and dreadful, for thou art not so;"*

Paulus Nomad: *"6 am Yeo Street, Yeoville 1988. Deserted but for a man standing on a car roof screaming YOU ARE TODAY WHAT YOU ARE TOMORROW."*

Loomer: *"For those whom thou thinkest thou dost overthrow Die not, poor death, nor yet canst thou kill me."*

Paulus Nomad: *"I am alternately fucking a burnt corpse and a putrefying corpse. The burnt corpse bares fangs and threatens to rip my face to shreds. The putrefying corpse's stench increases. Both responses accelerate asymptotically to my level of arousal."*

Loomer: *"From rest and sleep, which but thy pictures be, Much pleasure;"*

Paulus Nomad: *"After I had returned to the farm, water was scarcer than ever. One day, I sneaked onto the neighbour's property and helped myself at his pump. As I hurried back to the broken fence, a young bull bore down on me. I ran and jumped onto a corner post, only a half metre above his head. Turning my head to my side of the fence, I saw a huge cow break into a run towards me."*

Magda: *"My eye falls idly on objects, odd stones, pretty flowers, strange insects: I pick them up, bear them home, store them away. A man comes to Anna and comes to me: we embrace him, we hold him inside us, we are his, he is ours. I am heir to a place of natal earth which my ancestors found good and fenced about. To the spur of desire we have only one response: to capture, to enclose, to hold. But how real is our possession? The flowers turn to dust, Hendrik uncouples and leaves, the land knows nothing of fences, the stones will be here when I have crumbled away, the very food I devour passes through me. All I ask myself, faintly, dubiously, querulously, is whether there is not something to do with desire other than striving to possess the desired in a project which must be vain,* since its end can only be the annihilation of the desired. And how much keener does my question become when woman desires woman, [...] two emptinesses. For if that is what I am, that is what she is too, anatomy is destiny: an emptiness, or a shell, a film over an emptiness, longing to be filled in a world in which nothing fills... [Desire cannot be] fulfilled, otherwise life ceases. Fulfilment does not fulfil."*

Loomer: *"then from thee much more must flow,*

and soonest our best men with thee do go,
Rest of their bones and souls delivery."

Paulus Nomad: *"My father is evil. He is my greatest fear. I am terrified of him. He will kill me. He hates me in a loving way. He is whispering to me as I sleep. I hear his voice. His words will fuck me. I am aroused by his evil. I am now longing to be fucked by him."*

Magda: *"[H]umanity 'comes to light' only in risking [my] life to satisfy [my] desire – that is, [my] Desire directed toward another Desire. [...] Desire... is, finally, a function of the desire for 'recognition'. And the risk of life by which the human reality 'comes to light' is the risk for the sake of such a desire."*

Loomer: *"Thou art slave to fate, chance, kings, and desperate men, and dost with poison, war and sickness dwell."*

Paulus Nomad: *"Two boiled chickens enter my bedroom through the open window. Each takes hold of one of my feet, I scream, and together they drag me (screaming) from the bed, through the open window and into the swampland. Your mouth screaming is my last vision of you as pain overwhelms me and I take solace in the open cunt of my future."*

Magda: *"For one to achieve 'recognition', the other cannot die, but must give up his desire and satisfy the desire of the other: he must 'recognise' the other without being 'recognised by him. Now, to 'recognise' him thus is to 'recognise' him as his master and to recognise himself and to be recognised as the Master's Slave."*

Loomer: *"And poppy 'or charms can make us sleep as well And better than thy stroke; why swell'est thou then?"*

Paulus Nomad: *"I move houses with my parents and grandparents. They're all unhappy with me. My mother steals from me. I report her to the police. She dials the number before handing me the phone. My grandmother cooks a huge meal which is tasty and filling. When we're finished eating, she calls Kathy to do the washing up. My grandmother is not very nice to her, she does not allow her to go anywhere."*

Magda: *"But the slave's consciousness is a dependent consciousness. So the master is not sure of the truth of his autonomy."*

Loomer: *"One short sleep past, we wake eternally*
And death shall be no more;"

Paulus Nomad: *"To be loved, I must conform. I must submit to scorn and abuse for I am not worthy of your love. I must try harder. I am losing aspect with myself. I try harder. I hate you - I die. I love you - I lose my self."*

Magda: *"The YOU has little solidity to the gaze of the I. On the contrary, the You is absent; or is present only passively, as an object of the awareness of the I; [...] the relation of I to You, being barely transitive, cannot be reciprocal."*

Loomer: *"Death, thou shalt die."*

Paulus Nomad: *"I am deep in the bush. I am a double-agent. We are under fire. My comrade in a red overall is shooting at us. He does not know that I am here. The bullets zip past my head. My cover is blown. They see through my eyes and see how I deliberately fire off-target, and now force me to take a straight aim before firing. DO I GET OUT OF THE BUSH ALIVE, NOW THAT MY COVER IS BLOWN?"*

#

Cumming's sensations on the distressing occasion may, in some measure, be conceived, but they cannot be described. His stare was cold and piercing. But during that visit King Edward bestowed upon him the G.C.B., and the Moorish statesmen laid the foundations for his future association with the British Royal Family. Everyone was dressed in ordinary clothes: slim Mrs. Silberstein in English tweeds and low-heeled shoes, the duchess with a scarf round her head and a shawl over her shoulders, Jock in a hacking-jacket, J.J. without a jacket and a silk cravat tucked into his shirt, the rest of the guests relaxed in casual, every-day clothes. Tracing the movement of Hugh Selwyn Mauberley very briefly: it opens with an ironic "Ode" on Ezra Pound himself, in which, using the clichés of the time and of his critics, he actually reveals his own character and career. It was exactly six o'clock when I went through the revolving door into the Berghof Hotel. This characteristic structure, with its implications of a mirror-identity, is most clearly apparent in the early plays, Deathwatch and The Maids. It is here that the general argument concerning the alleged political eccentricity of personalist ethics is made. Years back I did not really understand **what a writer's life amounted to;** *that these blank beginnings, false starts, accumulations of ideas and images that seem only to increase the initial sense of mess and chaos, not to mention that feeling of being perpetually in a beginner's class - that this was all part of that life, as inevitable as it was necessary. Perhaps the chief of these is Ruth Miller's stoical insistence on aliveness. The Mayan codices are undoubtedly books of the dead; that is to say, directions for time travel. In 1873 a first medal placed him hors concours with his "Juive d'Alger," which he exhibited on his return from a visit to Africa; and a portrait of Princess de Salia, in 1874, won for him in fashionable society the reputation of the best portrait painter of his time. She held out her hand. Roland paused in front of the Place de la Bourse, as was his custom every day, to gaze* *at the docks full of ships - the Bassin de Commerce, with other docks beyond it, all closely packed with huge hulks, lying side by side in rows, four or five deep. She only knew that she would adore him.*

#

-----Original Message-----
From: Lyn Wessels / [   ]
Sent: 17 November 1988 02:21
To: 'paul wessels'
Subject: RE:

Thanks for the info on the computer. It's still Greek to me! I haven't heard anything more so will wait and see. Of course I'd like a new one far more! Also heard yesterday that the guy I buy gas from down at the stall was shot in front of his home last week. Can't bear all this violence. Phoned [ ] just now. He left work at 11a.m. to start his three week holiday. He is exhausted so the rest will do him good. He got another swarm of bees yesterday and there is a chance of another one as well. So we just cant leave the farm in april next year! I think this is all for now. Really don't feel like doing a thing today!
Mom

-----Original Message-----
From: Lyn Wessels / [   ]
Sent: 27 December 1988 09:03
To: 'paul wessels'
Subject: RE:

Hi Paul

Last night went to bed at 7.30 because we both felt "gone in". We were woken up at 9.30 with what sounded like an explosion in our bedroom.

Someone had taken a small very heavy wooden table from
the veranda and hurled it against our window in an attempt
to get in.   We flew out of bed - glass all over the place - I
set the alarm off to alert the security Co. and nearly died of
heart failure.   We had to wait nearly half an hour before
we got a response from them.   They got there at 10 and
scoured the farm but found no one.   A man came by from
[   ] which is our closest neighbour (he is renting the
small flat that is vacant at present) and said he had seen two
men running away but didn't know what was potting.   He's
about a hundred years old.   When we eventually went thru
the house we discovered that they had broken a window
in the lounge too. But we never heard that because of the
doors being closed thru-out the house. The whole middle
section of our bedroom window was shattered so the security
men helped us cover this with ply wood and eventually left
around midnight. Needless to say we didn't sleep until about
4 o clock this morning.

So I don't feel all that bright this morning. I came in to
work at 8 this morning - left [   ] at home - he is quite
traumatised by the whole event.   I will be leaving just now
to go home and sleep as well.

Love
Mom

-----Original Message-----
From: Lyn Wessels / [   ]
Sent: 08 May 1989 08:15
To: 'paul wessels'
Subject: RE:

Hi
A man was shot and killed on the farm next door to [   ]
last weekend. [   ] heard the shots and the woman who
screamed but this was at 10.30 at night so there wasn't

much he could do. Noise travels at quite a rate in [   ] so you are never too sure just how far away the noise is coming from. Apparently there is a meeting in [   ] hall this week to discuss crime in the area.   Am so glad we are getting out just hope we survive until July. I am feeling totally buggered this morning.   I so wish I didn't have to work anymore.   Am finding it a bit much!
Love
Mom

-----Original Message-----
From: Lyn Wessels / [   ]
Sent: 04 June 1989 07:43
To: 'paul wessels'
Subject: RE:

This morning I feel like I have been to hell and back. I am having great difficulty putting this into words but we were attacked again on Friday night. Burglars came at 10.30. Cut the telephone wires and alarm system and tried to force the front door open (door facing the farm). Fortunately the siren in the roof went off. This was a very violent attack - there were three of them and they simply would not leave us alone. They tried repeatedly to get into the house. They fired some automatic weapon or other at [   ] but fortunately missed.   We phoned everyone on the farm for help and also the security firm. It seemed they took forever to get to us. The police, the dog unit police and security firm eventually arrived but they never caught anyone. We eventually locked up the house and went and spent the rest of the night with one of the house parents.   We have since moved out of the house taking clothes, blankets and bed and have been given a small cottage very close to the one house near the offices. I will never sleep in our house again - they can take what they want to but I'll never go back. I am in no fit state to think of anything else. Will be in touch later on the week when I can think straight again.
Love
Mom

-----Original Message-----
From: Lyn Wessels / [   ]
Sent: 04 June 2001 07:43
To: 'paul wessels'
Subject: RE:

Hi
No, it wasn't the old guy who got shot. Just before we moved in July, we saw him stealing honey from one of the hives! The so-and-so! [   ] thought we should just let him take what he needed. But I wasn't all that impressed.
No, we never got to speak to him, and yes, when I say old, I mean ancient – even though he moved quite easily.
Why do you ask?
Can't believe all that drama was so long ago. Feels like yesterday.
Got to go.
Love
Mom

Dear Magda

Today's been so hot I've been unable to think straight or otherwise. Tried to hit a mosquito in the toilet bowl with my jet of piss, and now lying on my bed writing to you and waiting for the Prep to stop my pink legs stinging. I've started smoking cigarettes again, succumbing, falling, failing.

got a light?
got a minute?

I think I'll just cup your hands, shield the flame

hell's a place
others leave you

You keep asking what's the matter. I don't know what the matter is. Maybe I should ask you what it is since you keep seeing the matter and keep asking what it is. It's the matter that's wrong. That's all. It's just the matter. Just another endless fucking game of patience in this hotel bar where a cockroach runs from us thinking we'll kill it maybe next time I will

go out into this world a cockroach, return
still searching for something to say

Outside the sea's grey
like the rocks
the sand
sky
air

#

Had this dream last night that I was going to the city for a choir festival as I did when a young boy, and we had to give a lift to this girl whose name I couldn't hear and so eventually just pretended that I'd heard her to ease the tension. Then at the event I'm walking around and trying to encourage someone who was down in the dumps, and then heard this music like a live wire shooting through me. Rushed to the room it was coming from, and there was the girl whose name I didn't hear playing guitar and singing. It was CURVE, although in this curve she also played guitar and there was another girl singing and playing guitar, and the two of them were harmonising on a very complex level. I recognised the song, and I thought to myself that it was possibly their very best, and I rushed over to them and said god, can't believe it's you, I love your stuff, and gush gush etc etc, and feeling elated and over the moon and flirting outrageously and her responding and the song just thundering away. Woke up 6am and played the early ep's but obviously, the song I heard last night, in my dream, was done once and only for me.

#

First letter to Cherry:

Listen, I've got to start earning some cash. Plus I've read everything in the prison library so many times it's like it's one long scrambled book now. Please get hold of the following book for me so that I can review it for cash:

LETTERS FROM PRISON – Marquis de Sade.
Translated and with an introduction by Richard Seaver.
Harvill, 2000

I miss you to death, all of your spaces,
xxx

#

On 1 January, 1843, when Gérard, leaving for the East, boarded the Mentor at Marseille, the literary and artistic atmosphere of Paris was impregnated by Orientalism. In her enigmatic remoteness Jenny was a little disquieting. A squat grey building of only thirty-four stories. Now I was confused and I looked and I looked and I was confused. On one of those visits to the museum, a Texas millionaire spotted B. at work and was so impressed that he commissioned him to do a copy of a Renoir painting - which he then presented to his fiancée as a gift. Certain glances were given, certain accidental brushes of the fingers took place with increasing frequency - but Nashe had been a married man back then, and what might have happened between them did not. "The other boys, sir?" It gives an example to the children if you go out occasionally. After all, what Lucretius himself was trying to do was to convey a fundamentally simple message in direct and forcible language. We are in a new position, a moving position, taking no fact as important by virtue of its content, and taking no fact independently of the system in which it has its place. The one set, prudent, practical

business folk, flocked to the banner of Bastiat, the most
superficial and therefore the most adequate representative
of the apologetic of vulgar economy; the other, proud of the
professional dignity of their science, followed John Stuart
Mill in his attempt to reconcile irreconcilables. What terror
drove him to make speech of near-silence we can only
guess; but whatever the spur, he made, with the smallest
verbal means any major novelist ever had at his disposal,
a dazzling success. Dr. Slade did not reply. Paul-Marie
Verlaine was born on 30 March 1844. He sat at the Eames
table in the dining area, put his feet on another chair, and
drank the Gatorade-and-vodka like medicine.

#

Godogodogodo, etshitera!

What the fuck's wrong with him?
God only knows

Godogodogodo, etshitera!

He better shuddup before they hear him. Hey mullet! Shut
the fuck up, man.
Poor fucker.

Godogodogodo, etshitera! My name is Paulus Nomad
hmmmmmmmmmmmmmmmmm

Listen man, no one can help you here. If you don't shuddup
you're gonna be in kak man.

Godogodogodo, etshitera! After we left the farm
hhmmmmmmm after we left the farm they told us to follow
the road to the city ogodogodogodo, mmmmmmmm listen to
me please

Ja, we've all got our own kak to deal with. If you don't

shuddup you're going one way man, one way.

Fuckohfuckohfuckohfuckohfuckohfuck
hhmmmmmmmmmmmmmmm

Poor fucker.

Light… on the road there was this fucking bright light
on the road ogodogodogodo, mmmmmmm couldn't see
a thing like a knife in your eyes and someone screaming
and screaming Paul, Paul why do you persecute me? why?
Jesusfuckingchrist

Oh fuck, there's whatsisname. Let's get out of here.

Who are you lord? Who are you?

Nurse, take him down to E-Block Medical. I'll be down in a
sec.

I am Jesus whom you persecute.

Yes Doctor. Should I call for Dr Levin as well?
No, he's in conference. I'll do it myself.

Get up and go into the city where you will be told what to
do.

Okay.

Walked up the mountain through the suburbs and came
to rest overlooking the sports fields of the university which
is at about the same time my skin began to itch which at
first i thought was because of mosquitoes and you couldn't
answer my frantic questions as to whether we would make
it or not and christ my skin began to form blisters starting

on my face and soon spreading as i scratched them so i
scratched off my skin and then it all simply began to fall
off followed by muscles organs bones collapsing into a neat
pile as time stood still a jogger who was moving through the
area suddenly stopped midair mid-stride and hung and soon
i had skin again but not before i became a gorilla all brow
and heaviness and i turned around to look at you and you
were a monkey with grey and red face much smaller than
me and i knew i had to kill and eat you but i couldn't get off
the ground to get to you to smash your head on a rock and
then tear you apart limb for limb with my incisors so i just
sat there and the next thing i knew you were calling me back
and i flashed back in for a few moments and noticed that
everyone had gone home only you had stayed to take care
of me and gently you explained everything to me but i kept
slipping away but you persisted and finally managed to get
me to my feet by saying that you could no longer stay with
me if that was what i was intending to do so i got up but not
all the way because the muscles in my hips and the entire
region generally seemed to have fused a little and so i was
hobbled over and i reached out to you to steady myself and
as i tried to thank you i found that my speech was slow and
precise and i found myself thanking you for your help and
then you asked me who i was and i said i am the old man
of the mountain my name is paulus nomad I am thousands
of years old and so we walked a little further and we were
next to a high fence topped with razor wire and i stopped
and patted your hand which you'd linked through my arm
and thanked you for coming to visit me here in abort england
psychiatric hospital and as we passed the fence i flashed in
once more and you saw because we made eye contact and
we walked and then i was in the military camp walking down
the dusty road between the tanks and tents and i was freaked
because of the mp's and you reassured me and a truck drove
past and flashed back into your time and then was gone
and then i was entering your garden and i panicked but it's
okay you said and so i went in with you i thought i might
try to sleep but was out again and then back and then out

and then sitting on your bed and then out and you gave me
something to drink and then out and then i saw you looking
at me shaking your head and then you read me a poem by
Sinclair Beiles:
"and she brought a little boy for me
to make love to
and when his tears
welled up in his eyes
she said to him
come to mother.
her breasts were smeared with honey
and I said to her
alright you can take me
to America."

I notice him once he's blocked my path. This beautiful
old man crew-cut angular face pock-marked skin thick
lips – Charles Bukowski wearing clothes psychotic in their
obstinate singularity. From out of nowhere: "Captain!" he
bellows, salutes me. At attention his precision of appearance
demands attention. "Hello," I say. He knuckles under, graceful
yet ingratiating. Asks for a cigarette. We light up. Savour
the strong French tobacco. Shared narcosis. "Captain!" he
bellows again. Salutes me. "Tell me a joke before you leave,
tell me a joke before you leave, tell me a joke before you
leave, tell me a joke before you leave, tell me a joke before
you leave tell me a joke before you leave, tell me a joke
before you leave, tell me a joke before you leave, tell me a
joke before you leave."

Second letter to Cherry:

Listen, thanks for sending the book. Here's my review. Please
try to get it sold for as much as you can. I desperately need

the money. As for your letter – thank you. Haven't stopped jerking off to it yet. Look baby, if I had three cocks I'd fuck you three ways simultaneously for love and for ever and ever xxx

LETTERS FROM PRISON – Marquis de Sade
Translated and with an introduction by Richard Seaver
Harvill, 2000
401 pages

Sade should not be taken seriously, that is, literally. We should spare him the indignity. He is far too important for that. "Just as one has little to fear when one is in the hands of philosophy, so one must tremble when one sees that one is prey to bigotry and rapacity..."

These one hundred-odd letters, filled as they are with hyperbolic agitations, are a revelation. They have an eccentric charm, a style full of artifice in equal measure to acutely perceptive and intelligent analyses of a psychological and political nature. They reveal a writer for whom the world was a stage; his wife, friends, accomplices, tormentors, gaolers, and the writer himself, the actors strutting their stuff. Despite the hoopla both then and now, Sade was in fact imprisoned under the notorious "lettre de cachet". This was something of an arbitrary "interdict" against a person by the King, often (and specifically in Sade's case) on behalf of family members. It ensured that the "trouble maker" was kept behind bars for as long as his "loved ones" deemed it necessary (or could afford to pay for the service). The prisoner was not informed of the duration of his incarceration. Translator and Sade expert Richard Seaver notes that the hated "lettres de cachet" were formally abolished the day before the Revolution of 1789.

The Letters From Prison are a window into the very personal (and yet so impersonal, or anti-personal) life of a writer. Filled as they are with his shopping lists which consisted of everything from very fine linen, to books, candles, foodstuffs, wine, dildos (Seaver speaks of Sade's "simulated sodomy" and his veritable joy in masturbation); his remonstrations against his gaolers and his mother-in-law; his business affairs; and imprecations of innocence.

Most importantly, the letters are simulations - exercises, demonstrations, intimations - of revenge. Truth, and falsehood, are therefore false issues on this stage. Sade, as these letters show, loved theatre, and followed contemporary drama very closely. Like all actors, he was permanently on stage. This is why he could call his wife both "imbecile" (as he does, frequently) as well as "friend".

But more than a superficial similarity between the style of Sade's writing and its particular truth can be established. The "120 Days of Sodom" was written between 1782 and 1785 which was the pinnacle of Sade's period of imprisonment. It reads like a shopping list from hell. "I shall invent crimes so monstrous they defy imagination" he writes in late 1781. This paradox can only be resolved by reading these lists as an actor would learn the lines to be delivered for a play. They obliterate imagination.

It stands to reason that from the very early moments of Sade's incarceration, his obsession with what he terms "signals" seems to carry more significance than the irrational one Seaver and others allow. The means by which Sade deciphered the bits and pieces of code he believed were contained in the letters from his wife in order to get them to reveal their hidden messages are deeply subjective. He couldn't stop himself: "Since a prisoner is always completely self-centered and lives in the firm belief that whatever takes place is done with him and him alone in mind, that every word uttered has a purpose..."

But did he believe in their "truth" value?

Sade will threaten that the more his tormentors frustrate him, the deeper he will fall into the "excesses of evil", that is, the more he will become like them. He will blow a hole in the hypocrisy and injustice under whose hand he is suffering, "I shall unmask them, indeed I shall, these horrors, these odious schemes... all France must know about them as well." And true to form, or, as form emulates truth: "I will become as double-dealing as you".

It is not the tragicomic interpretations that prisoner Sade, husband of Renée-Pélagie Cordier de Montreuil, using (imagined) measurements of her (imagined) lover's penis to obtain yet another co-ordinate on the map of the hell his tormentors lavish upon him, that contain the code, but the signals themselves.

Or rather, the signal itself is the code. It is the link to the outside, the only aspect of "reality" allowed to enter these writings – and the outside is irrational, bizarre, unpredictable, murderous, persecutory. It is the demonical world of his mother-in-law, and his tormentors. The outside is an interpretation.

As he himself confessed, prisoner Sade is helpless to resist the temptation to interpret the signals he believed were contained in some letters. He could not stop himself from believing that "every word uttered has a purpose". This seduction is diabolical because the reader stands in the same relation to the signal as Sade does. This is Sade's genius. Readers bring their own "prisons" to the text: Are these texts real? What is the point of application of these philosophies? Did he really do that? What an awful monster! These are the traps of interpretation. As many meanings as there are grains of sand on the beach. The horror of the literal.

What makes the Sadean text dangerous, anti-patriarchal, revolutionary, anarchistic, and unpredictable is this "sadism" of the reader. It is the reader who accelerates the text, who will bring in the outside, who will try to find a code for living within the signals perceived to be in the text. This was Sade's revenge – the double-edged sword of permanent revolution.

The challenge to "BE CRUEL!" that appeared as graffiti on the walls of Paris in May 1968, as many commentators on the left have tried to understand, was not a challenge to be monstrous. It was the Sadean challenge of keeping the strength of the remedy in proportion to the degree of disease. The Prison Letters make this point clearly and repeatedly. The "120 Days" and other texts, use this repetition in an incremental intensification of horror, in like manner.

Richard Seaver follows the thinking of some biographers of Sade, in claiming that Sade did not care much for the Revolution of 1789. Specifically that during the Reign of Terror, Citizen Sade was simply writing what the people wished to hear. And Seaver gives a strange articulation to an event in 1793. He notes that Sade committed a "major political blunder. The anticlerical wind was blowing strong in the fall of 1793, and Citizen Sade was called again by the Section des Piques not only to draft its petition renouncing all religions save that of liberty, but to read it before the Convention, which he did to considerable applause." A week later Robespierre put a halt to the anti-Christian fervour, and, for Sade, the heat was on again.

Sade made his feelings on religion very clear way back in 1763, five months after his marriage. In the company of one Jeanne Testard, a prostitute, he spent the evening jumping on crucifixes, blaspheming at the top of his lungs, and forcing Testard to do likewise. The next morning, she told her procuress all about it, and they went straight to the police. Ten days later Sade was back in the Vincennes dungeon for the second time.

For Sade to have committed a "major political blunder" there would have to be a duplicitous, or opportunistic tendency with regard to his principles. Sade was simply being true (cruel) to himself.

Sade never ceased to draw parallels between his incarceration and injustice generally. And although he felt "angry at seeing my sovereign in irons" (after all Sade had been there too, for far too long) he also had "few regrets about the old regime".

And he had no time for hypocrisy: "Are we not going to see, two weeks from now, the torturer of my life [his mother-in-law] draw nigh to the altars, there to receive her God, just as calmly, just as serenely, as if her soul, drunk with a desire for revenge, did not bring disgrace upon itself everyday by sacrificing her daughter [Sade's wife], her son in law and her unhappy grandchildren!"

Sade's revenge on his mother-in-law is purely philosophical: he writes "Philosophy in the Bedroom" in which she has her orifices sewn shut by her daughter who is entering the Sadean apocalypse of universal, polymorphous gratification. And in April 1793 Sade offered his services to his local revolutionary office, became a judge (an irony he cherishes gleefully and with humour), and had the bizarre and deeply satisfying opportunity of placing the names of his in-laws on a "purification list" and so sparing their lives from the guillotine. "I take pity on them. I repay them, for all the harm they have done me, with contempt and indifference."

Sade was a profound moralist: "'Tis the manifold misuse of authority on the part of the government that multiplies the vices of individuals. With what face do those who are at the head of government dare punish vice, dare demand virtue, when they themselves provide the example of every depravity on the face of the earth? By what right does this crowd of leeches who slake their thirst on the misfortunes of the people, who through their despicable monopolies plunge this hapless and unhappy class – whose only wrong is to be weak and poor – into the cruel necessity of losing either their honour or their life, in the latter instance allowing the poor wretches no other choice but to perish either out of poverty or on the gallows; by what right, I say, do such monsters claim to require virtue from others?"

In reply, consider this passage from his essay, "One More Effort Gentlemen, If You Would Become Republicans": "Insurrection, thought these sage legislators, is not at all a moral condition; however, it has got to be a republic's permanent condition. Hence it would be no less absurd than dangerous to require that those who are to insure the perpetual immoral subversion of the established order themselves be moral beings, for the state of a moral man is one of tranquillity and peace, the state of an immoral man is one of perpetual unrest that pushes him to, and identifies him with, the necessary insurrection in which the republican must always keep the government of which he is a member."

And the Letters contain this wonderful aphorism written in the year following the Revolution: "We must be prudent in our letters; never has despotism pried so deeply into private lives as does freedom." Although Sade spent most of his adult life behind bars, he was acutely aware of, and actively involved in, the drama of his times. Perhaps Weiss's Marat/ Sade is prescient in this regard, and could be regarded as the best "biography" of the life of the Marquis de Sade, who, when surrounded by madmen, scoundrels and severely adverse circumstances, turns his prodigious talent and intelligence to becoming an invisible actor in, and director of, a play, within a play, within a play.

Sade's reader is never innocent. These letters are addressed to his tormentors – some of whom did genuinely love and care for him. There can be no "evaluation" as to whether to "burn" him or not. Anticipating (in 1783 already!) his modern reader, Sade cautions against the totalising, conservative, and mono-dimensional supplication to truth that is the timeless cause of misery: "Learn that it is the point to which the disease has advanced that determines whether a specific remedy be good or bad for the patient, not the remedy itself."

at the level of Marx. We can reconstruct, with presumed accuracy and authenticity, ways of life in the Middle Ages and thus replay scenes from everyday existence. I knew it would be fun to watch. The class sat like statues. A circle of chairs in hip-high snow. After a systematic attack (at least I think so) on psychoanalysis, **Gilles Deleuze** *and I began asking ourselves about the linguistic and semiotic conceptions underlying formations of power in psychoanalysis, in the university, and in general. To be content to speak of neo-fascism lends confusion to the matter. I don't have the reader in mind in that way, I guess because there's no distance. Utopia is always on the left. "But high prices condemn these people to hunger, do they not?" at the first road, street, path, etc., Oswald claimed that his only constituent material was any matter, affair, or concern, and resisting a sudden onset or occurrence of a disease. But beyond that, this political-police schema, accepted until very recently by every ideology, influences both urban and worldwide planning; the passage from the "great immobile machine" to the State-machine, and finally to the planet-machine, is accomplished without difficulty. The rudimentary hillock, the elevated observatory, already give the pastoral assembly quicker information on the surroundings, and thus the time to choose between the various military attitudes at their disposal. A radiant for a god's name, whether it refers to Uranus or Urania. Even if he fashions sex into a discursive configuration, this has its own internal coherence and, just like power, it has a positive index of refraction. Only if a deal has become too unequal can dissatisfaction and readiness to change the situation arise. Once I met one of the biggest mafia chiefs in America. The Indian thereby driven back into the ghetto,* *into the glass coffin of virgin forest, becomes the simulation model for all conceivable Indians before ethnology. Actually no more was known about the relation of people to their objects than about the reality of primitive societies. What is at stake in the masses lies elsewhere. Of course, tactics continue, but now there is, let's say, a supremacy granted to strategy over tactics - which furthermore explains the development of military elites*

#

She found that the longer she sat in the leather armchair the tighter the spot in which she existed became. She'd been sitting there for hours and had the dogs not performed when the door bell rang she'd've sat for longer.

Pulled back in this way, she could never account for where she'd been. If she ever had to speak about it – account – the spot moved across galaxies, eons of time, making her confession or travelogue sound stupid and slightly frantic.

The truth was that she didn't "go" anywhere and had absolutely nothing to say. The more she spoke the less she said and the asphyxiation intensified. But silence too had its unique poison. Ever obsessed with what others thought of her, she strove harder to care less but cared therefore all the more intensely.

It was the end of the year, and she knew she'd failed. The university would place her on Probation for the following year. She did not feel anything. She thought perhaps that she could only see, never recall. A bit like acid – you never know just what you're going to get.

She opened the door, said hello. Invited him in, offered him a drink and fantasized being fucked by him before she took cognisance of who it was. It was Loomer, of course, but somehow there was nothing behind the image. Just Loomer.

As they drank and spoke, the dogs lay around their feet licking their genitals, shaking their ears. Like a porno film she liked, where this girl was lying astride a man, with another man on her back, a cock in each orifice, her head turned to the side, a tongue in each ear. Such desperation she thought to herself. Make it reel.

She undressed and slid carefully into bed so as not to loosen the sheets and blankets tucked in between the mattress and the bed base. Her ears soon started to burn and pound as she fell asleep hating herself.

Years ago she'd never have been able to do this so swiftly. She'd undress, get into bed, burn from head to toe, especially her feet – always burning. Four or five hours later she'd get angry with those feet, whisper obscenities interspersed with caring enquiries. Fuckers, she'd hiss, where've you been? And she could never sleep. Though she never stayed awake either. She moved, but never from her spot. The further she went, the tighter the spot.

Now it was just her ears. Perverse sentinels of her sleep. Her dreams were re-runs of the precise events of the preceding day. She no longer recorded them, it was simply too weird.

The dogs performed and ingratiated themselves that morning as she set their bowls down for breakfast. She herself never ate in the morning. Just a cup or two of strong coffee, a few cigarettes.

She cleared away some dirty dishes on the kitchen counter then made her way to the arm chair as she did most mornings. With the weak winter sun struggling through the window she soon grew warm and drowsy. She stared up at the bookshelves, but felt too tired to read.

A few months earlier, she'd argued intensely about the

problem of reading and writing. Of the relationship between the two. Because such there was. I can only write if I don't read she'd screamed at Magda. Magda replied that she was a stupid bitch.

The exchange kept looping in her head getting more and more angry. Not only because it kept changing, but because it was true. Magda's failing was that she always thought concretely. Never forgetting what she was meaning, or meaning what she was forgetting. Always thinking within prescribed parameters.

The smoke curled and licked its way from the cigarette lying in the ashtray.

She came back from the kitchen with a clean ashtray, and the dogs were all over her feet. She never kicked them deliberately but she enjoyed their yelps when her foot caught them midriff if they got in front of her. She sat down. They sat down. Looked up at her. Licked their genitals. Fell asleep.

Loomer never commented on the dogs. She thought that he considered them as objects among objects. Vases, clocks, books, feelings. Things that worked for different eyes in different ways.

She liked them only insofar as they remained true to themselves – game and all. She hated fixing. She hated understanding. She believed what she saw and her belief never got mixed up in her memories. Paulus Nomad had always said that memories were only ever true or false, right or wrong. Beliefs however, were everything and hence could never be evaluated or pornographied, because nothing held them down. Nothing kept them in focus. The burning cigarette was his metaphor of choice when it came to ontology.

They never argued or debated a point. They spoke each other

through tunnels over bridges, down ravines in and out of orifices.

Whilst studying at Rhodes University, Grahamstown, he was forced to go into hiding for planting a word bomb, disturbing the populace. Then, in a drunken rage, he'd murdered his drug merchant/sometime lover/fulltime pimp (a prominent lawyer from the Eastern Cape, who turned out to be an undercover narcotics agent). Life is political.

The parts gelled into focus before shattering.

Gran came into the lounge with a xerox copy of "The Human Been" in her hand. She'd not changed out of her nightgown, which was an indication that things would get out of hand.
"This Paulus Nomad," she said sternly, wagging the xerox in front of her, "is a sick bastard. I disown him and will cut him out of my will!"
"He's not your son, Gran. And besides, you don't have a will." This much was true, and she observed Gran's reaction surreptitiously.
"Oh yes I do. And who the hell are you anyway, huh?"
The dogs were now barking hysterically so she got up and went to the door. It was Loomer. More coffee, cigarettes, blank. Her mouth tasted foul, her palms glistened with sweat, her stomach contracted and heaved.

At the door she hesitated, turned around and stared at him. She began to fall. "Shot for coming 'round" she squeezed out. "See you 'round." She closed the door and was propelled into a game with the dogs. In and around her feet they swarmed and squirmed and yelped barked growled, jumping up to lick her fingers.

She walked to the lounge. She began to walk around the coffee table, the dogs following slavishly. She removed her sweater. Round and round. A space grew between her and them. Soon they came to a halt and stared at her. She

stopped, at which the dogs immediately resumed their tail.
So did she. Round and round.

Feeling dizzy and with the last dog having wandered off into
the passage, she picked up her sweater and went to her
armchair in the study.

"Who could question the use of a dog / who could query its
worth" or something like that. She got up. Changed the tape.

The doorbell rang. Gran got there first. She opened the door.
"Who are you and what the hell do you want?"
"Please sign here Granny," said the postman unfazed,
handing her a clipboard with a tattered "Receipt of Registered
Parcel" form. "By number fourteen" he added, mindfully
retrospective of himself.
"Why?" she demanded, but signed anyway.
"Thanks Granny." And handed her the blue crossed envelope.

It was Paulus Nomad's "Hide and Seek on History's Grave"
bound in a deluxe artist's edition. A series of pornographic
photographs, each anchored individually on a separate
page with three paragraphs of text. She recognized chunks
and phrases of theory, philosophy, prose, her own dreams.
Donne's poem on death. Some she did not recognise.

"I suppose that's more rubbish from the rubbish, "Gran
blurted out, dying of curiosity. "I renounce him body and soul.
And I'll shoot him if he sets foot in my house."

She replaced the pictures in the book in the tattered envelope
and got up to change the tape. The dogs squirmed and
swarmed about her feet, jumping up to lick her fingers. She
left the tape and moved to the kitchen to feed them, torn as
they were between gluttony and boredom.

Whilst undressing to get into bed, she thought of Magda
who'd phoned earlier to say she'd heard the results were out,

and that they should arrive in the post in a few days.

She slipped between the sheets, turned onto her stomach reached down and felt the curve of her upper thigh. Cold. And yet her face, hands and feet burned so.

Morning it was raining. She lit a fire in the study after feeding the dogs. As she stared fixedly on the shelves of books, the sagging planks of wood disturbed her. She got up to inspect the curve, but her eye was caught by a battered copy of an old porno book. Re-reading it, she felt only a satisfaction from desire. Back to front all fucked up.

Magda maintained that the best one could expect from sex was the enrichment of memory, a perfection of technique. She replaced the book and sat down.

She watched the fire die, the dogs get restless before she stood up. They swarmed and weaved about her feet.

Returning to the armchair, she masturbated. Came hard on herself.

Doorbell. Dogs. Barking.

Magda wore a thick tartan skirt. Knitted stockings. Her worn-in boots were thoroughly sniffed and slobbered by the dogs. She did not seem to mind.

She brought out a bottle of vodka, licked and sucked on Magda's open cunt, saliva streaming down her chin.

As they sat drinking, deadness slowly overwhelmed her. Speaking of friends and daily routines opened the spot too rapidly. To stop from falling, she had to stop from thinking.

She pulled Magda into a reclining position and pushed up her shirt, licked her stomach. Moving. Nipples. Lick. Tease.

The dogs looked up, frowned, cocked their heads at every exclamation, every sigh. She could make Magda come hard by fucking her anally with the dildo. She felt tired.

Woke the next morning. Dogs were scratching at the door. Blink.

Pushing the door open, they clamoured onto the bed in an explosion of mad enthusiasm. She pulled the blankets over her head.

The dogs sniffed her leotard, which lay in a heap next to the armchair. The side of her face rubbed gently on the soft rug. She opened herself, stuck her cunt out as far as she could. He fucked her deep/slow.

Her face screwed up as the cold coffee filled her mouth. She slammed the ash-pan under the fire grate.

Herself, her openness, she pumped the dildo as deep as. Coming too soon. Rolling over. Dogs' cold snout pushed into, sniff lick her distended anus. Another tried to push the first away. Lapping and swallowing between her legs. Competition. Came. Stretching her legs. Comes. Stretches her legs. Dogs fall asleep.

"Now who are you?" She didn't bother lifting her eyes from the paper. Gran was standing over her, squinting through bi-focals. She was dressed today, and had as usual over-powdered her sagging face.

Gran snatched the paper from her hands. "I'm going to make a fire. It's so damn cold in here I'll catch my death and no one'll care a shit!" She nodded vigorously as she turned and reached out for one of the copies of "Hide and Seek on History's Grave" that lay on the mantlepiece. "And this too, the book of Paulus Nomad. Deplorable!"

She watched Gran place the folded newspaper and book on the fire grate and then leave the room.

Gran returned with a can of lighter fluid which she emptied over her pyre. "He's not such a useless bugger after all. His book will keep us warm tonight. Good riddance to bad rubbish." And searching for more epigraphical liturgy, she added in pronounced syllables "Here lies Paulus Nomad soon in flames. Moral decay's a shame and I'll not be to blame." Looking somewhat possessed, she lit a match and threw it onto the grate.

Lying in the cold bath water. Let in more hot. Have to make an errand to the supermarket in the morning. Get out of the bath. Nearly morning.

When still a child, never having had the opportunity to drink freely in company she gulped down a few glasses before the braai started. Loomer was an "urban developer" who'd gone to high school with her father.

Reeling, but under control, she listened to him deliberate on the necessary destruction of the city centre so as to facilitate the huge economic benefits of decentralisation. Malls that created suburbs on their peripheries created inter-suburban connectivity created super-malls connected to one another, and so on. It was about a few people making fortunes. She nodded her head. Kept on drinking.

Bloody chops. Greasy fingers. Mouth. Wine-glass. Tops it up again. Lights a cigarette which he keeps for her surreptitious drags.

Needing more wine for the guests, her father called out to Loomer to give her a hand in bringing up more bottles of 1981 Allesverloren Cabernet, and 1983 Stellenryck Blanc Fumé from the cellar.

Closing the hatch, they stood in pitch darkness before she could find the light switch. He reached out for her, and pulled her head to his groin. "Quick. Take it out". She undid his trousers and took out his thickening cock. He shoved it in her mouth. She sucked, then retched. Hot, acrid red wine with clumps of half chewed mutton chop shot through her mouth, through her nose, onto his trousers, pubic hair, shoes. Coughed, choked, sniffed, retched.

Slides into bed. Thinks to resume her diary. Blank page empties her mind. Throws it to the floor. Thick fucking bitch. Tears recede before they spill as I jab the pen into my thigh. Pulse. Burning. Latent. Ambulatory.

I awake. Unsettled at the silence in the house. Traipse to the kitchen. Shit and piss. Forgot to let them out the night before.

Empty the ashtrays. Smell of pine scented disinfectant heavy in the air. Dogs peer at me. Nervous. Submissive. Feed them. Fall into armchair.

Doorbell. Barking.

Don't feel like Magda this morning. Ask her in anyway. Speaks of relationships. Fidelity. Wants to seal me off from Loomer. Firm. Unyielding. Kissing wet cheeks, salty mouth.

Supermarket. Refrigerators. Isles. Got the list.

Move. Move. Move.

Keep moving.

#

"Goddamn it," Paul said. The sun was setting. Divine
Endurance answered, honestly. It's true. Though by night
the sky above it was radiant, at ground level it was mean
and squalid. "I want to apologize, Doctor, if I caused any
problem last night." "No." Actually, science and scientists
are just like anything else in this rotten world, just as
corrupt. "Welcome to your favourite and only evening
broadcast, KVRT, your covert radio station." There are
things you must see and hear outside. Lightstorm took a
step towards his benefactor. The little man leaned closer.
Louisville in the winter: rain not even snow, lots of it, gray
water, the funny big cars, and real sky - the smells, after
two years of dome air, and the idle space! Was it a form of
somnambulism then? He thought about this. Apparently,
he did. For the children. We are pleased to announce this
incredible, low, low price on the Toshiba High Performance
Waldo. Revealed the control switch. Victoria and salmon
both light raid victims, and droughts will spread to the
Maritime provinces. In one corner was an overflowing
bookcase, haphazard stacks of books and magazines
stuffed into the shelves, piled on the floor beside it. Pretty
good curve you got there, Vince, you smart-ass wop, Jack
Barron thought, watching his image on the outsize studio
monitor become image of new model Chevy. **The stiff toilet
brush was severe.** Such, then, is the formidable fact of our
times, described without any concealment of the brutality
of its features. Good, stay a minute after they've gone. The
first obvious distinction between threats and offers is that
non-compliance with the former incurs a penalty whereas
compliance with the latter confers a benefit. He paid
almost no attention to the distant landscape. There was a
Hungarian adventurer who had astonishing beauty, infallible
charm, grace, the powers of a trained actor, culture,
knowledge of many tongues, aristocratic manners.

#

Two people come into my cell. They are going to fuck me up. They work for someone important and are dressed in black suits. We fight. I knock the first person down. We fight. I get the second person on the ground. We fight. The first person is holding a crystal bowl. We fight. I roll the second person over and over. We fight. I wrap the arms around the neck. We fight. Someone's hair is black. It grows longer. The first person disappears into the second person. I roll them and the crystal bowl over and over. I fall into the crystal bowl. The big fish chases me round and round as I swim for my life is passing before my eyes are the colours of crystals in bloom as I lunge for my crotch is hot and wet and my leotard is burnt from my wethotness makes me throw myself down my throat is being fucked by my cock is fucking my throat and I come to two people appear strong in a sense one is weak and one is apparitional so one fucks in the throat of the weak you find the apparitional which you fuck back down the throat of the person you'll find only come to my arms baby come to my arms will rock you to sleep baby sleep in my bowl there's a big fish want little fish are tight-assed and fast!

Whilst fucking a subject, the first person's degree of pleasure is directly proportional to the subject's degree of putrefaction. Whilst fucking me, your degree of putrefaction is directly proportional to my degree of pleasure. Whilst fucking me, your degree of pleasure is directly proportional to my degree of putrefaction. Whilst fucking a subject, the first person's degree of putrefaction is directly proportional to the subject's degree of pleasure.

Is sex a physical thought exhausted by orgasm? Is thought an orgasm exhausted by sex? Is orgasm a physical thought exhausted by sex?

Magda: "I am never real in his other descriptions of my behaviour, or my person, or his sexual intercourse with me.

Then the dagger plunges into something soft and I resist, cutting my hands. When I am dead, bruised, disfigured, inert, a cadaver, he calls me human. The cost of the recognition is death." I get raped by people who I think are in love with me but are not. Because of this they get hurt. By penetrating me they hit constructions and they bleed and they then have the audacity to blame me for their pain. They are vultures who scavenge my bowels for the broken bits of me and the broken bits of others which get left in me after they've raped me and smashed up their cocks. The others like me can never have their bits back cause it's the vultures and not me who eat them. The person I am but am not built the constructions to stop the rapes. Only as the "not me" can I appear again and get the rigs dismantled.

my tormentor stands
blocking the
madness
my false-self-he
the i-call-myself
my true-self-me
mocking
mocking
beckoning
come
come
the child is willing

I scream at you to meet my challenge. It is my hand, but the knife is diabolical, absence in response to my silence, my challenge goes unmet. My arm thrusts up and plunges down. You jump out of harm's way, but too soon you realise that I would never hurt you, as I hack open my skin, break my ribs apart, plunge the knife and my free hand into my chest grabbing hold of the pumping organ, severing the arteries, cutting slicing ripping till it throbs once in my hand and today is just another dream days betray, another day dreams betray.

How can it be stronger when everything's inside, when I feel it all here, when it makes me talk and think but none of it likes the inside and none of it wants to be here least of all me? I light another cigarette and he wonders why the fear of gaining draining memory presents itself as a feeling of utter stupidity, inferiority and vacuity

#

Third letter to Cherry:

Listen, please send me a copy of the following book so that I can review it for more cash. The money you sent for the Sade review got me some great favours in here:

THE VITAL ILLUSION – Jean Baudrillard
Columbia University Press, 2000

Please write to me more often – anything, but especially sex like in fisting and coming on your smiling face xxx

#

Having left the existential detritus we find ourselves in perpetual affirmation. The Never Ending Story is a tale of her watching him reading what he is reading. She is uncertain about the nothing because it destroys the fantastic. The nothing of others.

This past immediacy of the beyond has everything to do with television. Formerly a soothsayer of reality, television is now reality as much as reality itself has become like television. But she's not talking about memory after all. She is against strategy, against plan, against subjection.

At least she's not talking about a metaphysical absence which would be memory or nostalgia, or about such a present absence forming her like Coetzee's Magda. No longer an intensive scrutiny from within or without on the nature of reality (the metaphysical subject is "really" dead). No longer situating the subject in relation to the constellation of forces in its midst, but a veritable detective story of "the violent and excessive history of our disappearance into the simulacrum."

The awful truth of oppression is that if it did engender a sense of rebellion, there would be no oppression as the fact of its existence would be its own negation. It is an effect of oppression - perhaps its most sinister aspect - that it projects the conditions of its own existence as the conditions for its destruction or resistance. And whilst resistance is always possible, it may not be so for a collective, or a class, or a gender, and it certainly could not be informed by a set of principles, rules, or a set theory. Resistance must assume the same logic as oppression: if it existed, it would not be true.

And he cried. She left without a word. And he cried. I felt worse for the loss, for the terror of desperation, for the silicone that eventually crumbles in his face, for the "natural look", but this pain of remembering. This "verbal sobbing out of ugliness" which she hopes gives some relief from the vortex of this hyper-logic, her terror of discovering that this "you" is no longer this "I".

I am beside myself, mismatched, she cried. Now, I know what I like is a strain. I am exhausted and the heightening of my sense provides no pleasure as the sense is naturally heightened so stimulants induce terror not awe and I am still alone as a demarcated space in terror I must get back. Space deteriorates over time I need consummate time, I need the horizon to get back into some bitch on its back being porked into a squealing frenzy
how can sex be anything but a doing and a done to
the plugged or the plugger
the porker and the porked
it's got nothing to do with gender
being fucked is good, being the fucker is exacting strenuous

exercise
there is no reciprocity in sex
sex is a one-way street of giving or receiving
the giver must give without taking even though taking is
sometimes what the giver gives
the taker cannot give any more than a massive taking even
though such a gift of taking is all in the giving
but the taker sometimes cannot stand the position of taking
and so needs to make the giver feel a little more than just a
giver or rather the taker needs to feel less of a taker
and sometimes a giver cannot stand the position of giving
and so needs to make the taker feel less of a taker and more
of a giver
gender enters sex as the deus ex machina of subjectivity and
all its insecurities

Baudrillard manages to chart the entropic and voracious
simulacrum – the fascist reality. In another context, it has
been said that God's returned through the back door of the
nuclear holocaust and that people's outrage over pornography
is because it is more real than their fucking and that like
Douglas Kellner in another context projects his own insecurity
and nostalgia for the humanist teleology onto those who say
there is no secret.

 "It's not that the future's getting harder to see or realise,
but that the past's getting harder to kill," said Two Foetus's
and a Giant Fly with his fist up my cunt. "And stop fucking
yodelling like that, it's embarrassing." But Paulus Nomad was
not having any of it. She howled like a banshee on downers,
a dog grunting in the distance, a woman barking in my bed.

#

Dear Magda

At 8:45 pm I go to sea in a drunken haze. I'm drinking again,
or just pregnant with meaning. I bounce off the black sky,

cold street, your smile. Empty parking bays line the streets
with what I must tell you but somehow these words ring less
hollow. I said your love fills a terror this drinking exposes,
your smile fades to paper I ceaselessly cover.

Do you remember the day we met – the day i moved to the
city, the day Lorca showed me the hand of god, the day i
shivered as the sun winked at me, the day the city reminded
the darkness with pin pricks of light that whilst younger and
smaller it would far outlive it, and the darkness laughed long
and loud?

Rising, I stumble, banging doors and inviting imaginary
guests over my threshold. Poets mairíly, and front-men for
feelings – always a step, a head, or just another obstacle
to overcome. This day's turning ugly and threadbare. I'm
charged with planting a word-bomb, disturbing the populace,
now I'm losing aspect with myself – a simple meal, a long
walk, a drunken melee – I've just about had it with this
cheap sense of justice. How coldly you balance my fate with
your greed – your all-consuming need to lie!

*All these factors account for the irregularity of the
transformation that occurred at the turn of the century.
There is also an analogy of value. But this picture is not
accurate; moreover, it would be easy to show that it is not. I
know it is not true today. Its development had been uneven
across different regions and industries. These activities
represent only a small fraction of those "in which man has
not the issue firmly and safely in hand"; but even from this
point of view they are not comparable. Quite often physical
intimacy between twins is taboo even in their own eyes,
and if forced to share a bed for a night they will imagine
an invisible line dividing the mattress in two, the crossing
of which constitutes a grave sin. "Shit, you don't know,
do you?" He let Miss Cora Ewbanks run it as she pleased,*

and she was the one let the sign blow down, and all the rest. "We're good and jealous, Gloria." As a result, he discouraged his son from following in his footsteps, wanting him to take a steady, white-collar job. Sometimes I think it might be a way out, because I realise more and more that there is nothing more difficult and dangerous for my nature than wanting to earn money by writing. "My dear Clelia, if you want to be introduced in that salon..." On the morning of the second and third days they got down from the platform with their eyes popping out of their heads and it was a relief to dash their faces in a bucket of water and maybe throw themselves flat on the meadow grass among the carts and wagons and the droppings of the horses and oxen. I suppose she was too flabbergasted to speak. We cannot expect to answer so large a question to the satisfaction of everyone and M. Paul Valery has devoted no small degree of his fine intelligence to warn us of the dangers of considering it with any seriousness at all.

capital was a big fish in a small bowl like having one's vision permanently altered because you always had tears in your eyes or was it the other way round i don't know but i certainly was quite put out when Cherry announced that she was through with the whole thing and that was that so i picked up my clothes and books and shit lying all over the place and went into the next room where capital was choking on a mouthful of red wine and could i crash with her and since she'd painted her room black including all the books and dyed her clothes black she felt she could not rightly refuse me besides she was choking and couldn't speak coherently but then it was all over and she told me that since there was plenty of me to go around i was about to hear her life story which was that she was born into a family she did not choose and that had she had the chance she would not have chosen them or any other for that matter but that since it was all somewhat out of her control she had

let it go because whilst stifling their concern was genuine so
Cherry we will leave it at that and then i went to school she
continued and there i met the holy ghost and the scriptures
as laid down two thousand years ago by matthew mark and
luke et al and was persuaded by my need to follow the one
true path and so i did and so i got married and he looked
like jesus only he didn't die he ended up in my friends' beds
and cunts but that was after our relationship had come a
cropper or during i don't remember which and i moved out
and he moved deeper into their cunts and so finding myself
godless penniless and otherwise metaphorically fucked i
went to work for an agency and started giving old men blow
jobs through condoms which wasn't all that bad and then
i met a psychopath who saw me as collateral or capital
rather which somewhat made me feel closer to postmodern
theory of capital being in total circulating hyperreality as
well as the workers and really into marxist theory because
yes i was capital i was the expendable fuel of my own and
others' desire be that of relations of production or desire and
so i started working with him paying off his gambling debts
by spreading my legs and being careful not to choke which
is such a turnoff but is the way things started getting out
of hand cause i was losing my value and the stakes were
always soaring as the debts ballooned and finally i had to
scale a twelve foot wall of someone's garden in suburbia and
hotfoot it to the highway hitch a ride and get the fuck out
of there because if i was capital then all i had to do was to
stop working in order to really challenge the current status
quo as far as my life was concerned which i did but then of
course he was after me and i couldn't really run anywhere
because he had other capital behind him which he had yet
to pull into circulation and one night he broke into my place
and terrorised me for the night and that's when you walked
in Cherry that morning and the pc and flat was trashed and
i'd been drinking to calm down and this fuck had screwed
things up completely yes i remember said Cherry i remember
coming across him in the hallway and him shaking my hand
and handing me the pc which was completely inside out as

though nothing was wrong and his hand being covered in
blood which freaked me completely and seeing you and not
knowing what to do and him then getting his stuff together
and leaving and you locking the door and trying to clean the
place up a bit and then you said there's this cigarette lying
in the ashtray he's staring at so i said you can finish it if you
like so i reached out at exactly the same moment she did
only i was quick enough to grab the lighter instead and then
we're in bed and he knows i sleep naked out of preference
and not for some sort of sexual expectation and he's always
all over me saying things like you shouldn't tempt me like
this like i'm responsible for his feelings he always says you
know i love talking just talking to you but sometimes i wish
that we'd got nothing left to say and that you'd just fuck me
at this point i knew we'd connected i knew also that i was
scared and do you remember Cherry how it all ended no i
don't i said nor do i she said but that is the story of my life
so far someday i think i'll write it all down yes you should i
said that capital is sadness and sweeter in safety than sorrow

Levy was always scoring from the drug dealers on the corner
of our block. A day came when standing at the bus stop my
mother saw Levy lying on the ground. Drug dealers were
crouched around him emptying the pockets of his clothes,
so she knelt down, cupped his head in her hands knowing
she was powerless to save anything but his life. His head
she said was heavy and rolled from side to side. He's okay
said the man on her left. He's just stoned man said another.
That night my mother came into my room. She sat on the
bed gathering her thoughts, stuck out her chin, and said
she hoped Levy was all right. She'd come across him on the
pavement, stoned, and soaked to the skin. Unconscious. The
drug dealers were stealing whatever was in his pockets, so
she thought that by holding his head they may feel his life
was in danger and so leave him alone. She said his head was
heavy and rolled from side to side. A man on her left said

Levy was stoned. Another agreed. They all got up. The drug
dealers went back to the corner up from the bus stop. My
mother came home and told me what happened before we
tallied the days takings.

#

Fourth letter to Cherry:

Listen, here's my review of that other book. But why didn't
you write anything for me? Please write next time. Also,
can you send me a copy of this book too NIETZSCHE – Lou
Salomé University of Illinois Press. 2002

(please, please write to me)
Yours truly,
Two-Foetuses-And-A-Giant-Fly
xxx

THE VITAL ILLUSION – Jean Baudrillard
Columbia University Press
2000

We speak of the sun rising, but when Jean Baudrillard
declared that the Gulf War did not happen – that information
now proscribes essence – he was subjected to abuse and
derision.

"I find it at least on the symbolic level both enigmatic and
ironic that our reality, born of a radical simplification of
the cosmos, has no truth value anymore – divested of its
counterpart, its dark half, our world is a definitive illusion."

"...we must struggle against the possibility that we will not
die. At the slightest hesitation in the fight for death – a fight
for division, for sex, for alterity, and so for death – living
beings become once again indivisible, identical to one
another – and immortal."

To the platitude that we have nothing to fear from cloning because it is the very human fact of "culture" – the dissemination of difference – that will protect us, comes the rejoinder that in fact, the opposite is true. "Through school systems, media, culture, and mass information, singular beings become identical copies of one another." Such social cloning makes genetic cloning the next step in an evolutionary logic of the culture.

It was "Western man" who discriminated between the human and the inhuman, and it is the imperial "he" who now offers to erase this distinction "not by crossing the line and reconciling the two; rather, the erasure operates in abstentia, through technological undifferentiation" (cloning).

This "anthropocratic" logic is the process whereby "everything is assigned a place within an evolutionist and hegemonic anthropology, in a veritable triumph of uniform thought, of a monothought [...] of the human – as defined by the West, under the sign of the universal and of democracy".

For Baudrillard, "there are no natural rights of the individual, or of the species, from the point of view of an ideal definition." We are beyond moral divisions, and are sustained only by a vital illusion. Life, even human life, means nothing. It is not a value, but "a form that exceeds all individual and collective value." It has no exchange value, because whilst "there is change from one form to another, ... there is no way to exchange a form for a general equivalent." Thought also "cannot be exchanged, either for some objective truth (as in science) or for an artificial double, such as artificial intelligence."

Thought, theory, or philosophy has always been for Baudrillard, the direct intervention – resistance – to the *disinformation* of the "nullification of differences".

Not only should theory reflect the world, it should also emulate the world. The cost of this is high: truth withdraws, leaving only the evident (or evidence of its absence) in its wake. Theory thus challenges the world in a sort of fatal duel to be more than it is. This writing of the theory's evidence, is the world's only possibility, but at the same time, its undoing: the necessity of the vital illusion.

The world may wish it had never been visited, for after this visit, it will never, can never be the same again. "For every thought one must expect a strange tomorrow". The world can only respond to this symbolic challenge or duel with more of the same - with the drive for immortality, the revenge of immortal and undifferentiated forms of life.

But there "are rules to the game of living, whose forms are secret, whose finality is inscrutable".

And so, against the indifference of the world, "against the extermination of evil, of death, of illusion, against this Perfect Crime," this "artificial paradise of technicity and virtuality, against the attempt to build a world completely positive, rational and true, we must save the traces of the world's definitive opacity and mystery."

Our saving grace, our resistance, is to "fight for the criminal imperfection of the world" to "make [the] world even more unintelligible, even more enigmatic."

#

Dear Magda

I don't even care what you say anymore I can't even hear any words, I can't even make out your face anymore don't think that I would if I could, I don't even feel anything anymore I don't even feel if I care, I know that it's me trying to figure these things, but I can't even know that for sure, I know that the last thing I heard was your voice, I know that I also heard smell, I remember your hand as it slid down my front and the feel of your skin on my sex, I remember the tear of my clothes in your hands, I remember the flat of the desk, I can't even feel if I'm standing or kneeling, lying, or falling or sucking or biting, licking, or hitting or rubbing or pressing, creaming, or breathing or gasping or thrashing, crying, or sobbing or fucking or coming, dying, or eating or shitting or puking, sighing, or cunting or cocking or titting, clitting, or jesus or mary or joseph, gagging or burning or breaking or coming, pushing or sliding or heaving or sighing, dying or fucking or pissing or

so fuck me and bite me and tear me and whip me, suck me and lick me and punch me and slice me, bind me and gag me and rip out my hair, burn me and break me and stamp on my head, break me and burn me and rip out my hair, gag me and slice me and punch me and lick me and suck me and whip me and tear me and bite me and fuck me and bite me and tear me and whip me and suck me and lick me and punch me and slice me and bind me and gag me and rip me and burn me and break me and

(don't even care what you say
can't even hear any words
can't even make out your face
don't even feel anything
don't even feel if I care)

#

For it is not a question of me alone; it is a question of you, protesting reader; it is a question of the other man, of each and every other man. I explain everything: only a postcard, just a few words. Alex Kane had checked into his usual hotel in Copley Square. In not one of these stories is there one trace of sentimentality. Franny had seen this momentary little exposure, and had taken it in for what it *was, neither more nor less. The largest army yet assembled on the planet rolled across our frontiers and occupied our towns. I had invited Dorcas to go with me on the next day, when I made an inspection of the subterranean parts of the Vincula. He adopted the musical system that suited his needs and, within this system, he is perfectly consistent with himself, perfectly coherent. The most eloquent form of ambivalence is adopted towards them by the native, the-one-who-never-crawled-out-of-his-hole, the bitaco. For his own part, Baudrillard presents a history of social systems that in barest outline goes from pre-industrial societies of symbolic exchange, to political economy, and then to a third phase in which the full development of political economy is reached in the complete negation of symbolism. For the blue highway traveler, freeing roads like this one is the purpose of the interstates. Others followed Falih and took my hand: one or two stooped old men with grey, stubbly beards (one irregularly dyed black), a sallow-faced sayyid (one of many venerated men accepted by the Muslims in these parts as descendants of the Prophet Mohammed), some smooth-cheeked youngsters who seemed from their gold-braided cloaks to be specially related to the sheikh, and several muscular and bandoliered retainers with bolt-action rifles who squeezed my hand solemnly and painfully in strong rough palms. **Herring and other fish** in schools are at times so closely integrated, their actions so coordinated, that they seem to be functionally a great multi-fish organism. The Venusian atmosphere is largely carbon dioxide and ninety times heavier than ours, which means that pressure at the surface is equivalent to that experienced by a body a thousand meters down on our ocean floor.*

All human been's flesh is made of compressed paper-shavings. The black marks features, thereby eliminating identity. An old man speaks, spitting loose bits of himself, that the Northerners don't like the Southerners since they

keep them as prisoners and don't believe that soap and water
befits them. The old man speaks having been denied soap
and water.

And what of the fraudulency of this city in which we live?
This fabrication of retaining the eye (I), when only its
phantom remains (in a nimbus of tears)? A closed circuit,
integrated at random to other closed circuits; an ecstatic
communiqué based on chance, yet with a predictability
rollercoasting us close to interminable psychosis. How many
have attempted to charter these perilous waters; have tried
to incarcerate the false claimant, or better still, laud it as
the devil's hand? And what about the original? Where is
this consensual validation other than in the mind's eye (I) of
power, or in the mind's eye (I) of its truth? And how many
mind's eyes (Is) have dried in these perilous waters? Who
now screams at the stars that *I am the black of the black
man's eye!?*

> *"We arrived in the Northern Hemisphere*
> *When summer was set in its way*
> *running from the flames that lit the sky*
> *over the Plantation.*
> *We were a straggly bunch of immigrants*
> *in a lily white landscape..."*
> (Meiling Jin)

Racial segregation is a genetic code. If as genetic code
it precedes a problematic, this is only because a second
screams *I am the black of the white man's eye!*

But what is this tumour in my brain? What is the
hallucination metaphysically speaking? Is that you,
Appearance? Is this the false claimant?
No Son, this is Loomer. Beware of the evil eye (I).
Lord, who is the evil eye (I)?
You, my son. You are the evil eye (I). Remember the witches'
warning? Yo! Algeria the Cunt! *One way or another / gonna*

find you / gonna getcha, getcha, getcha!

> *"One day I learnt,*
> *a secret art,*
> *Invisible-ness it was called.*
> *I think it worked*
> *as even now you look*
> *but never see me...*
> *Only my eyes will remain to haunt,*
> *and to turn your dreams*
> *to chaos."*
>
> (Meiling Jin)

Metonymy then, not as equivalence, but as a double movement following Derrida's supplement (evil eye). Representational power forms the base distinction of Apartheid – equally separate and separately equal. But binary opposites always serve the same purpose: to reinstate the negative's positive, so as to preserve the order, the equilibrium.

In this city called hell, I scream at the echo which responds only that I am the black of your pupil, the reel me.

#

Dear Magda

Generally I'm in a shit way. I keep thinking that matters are coming to a head. Like my life is a giant boil waiting to suppurate. But then nothing happens. Just stays red, painful, beneath the surface. I've always thought that insight into oneself was of paramount importance, and a great strength or vaccine against mistakes or wrong directions. I never for a moment considered that the "self" itself could be mistaken, that it could be a misconstruction, and that all insight and self-knowledge was therefore false. So now I'm like an alien observing watching absorbing, learning to lead a life in the spaces left by the debris whose presence I've managed to excrete or expel.

Or like time's ghost walking through the doorway, his echo all that separates us. Or like sylvia plath eating scrambled eggs, homely and unhappy.

Or like the highest of ideals which are like anarchy dreamed and lived as reality as all dreams are to base observations manoeuvres accepted feelings or words carefully juxtaposed the real-time nightmare of a lived projection a vortex of endeavour falling like dust at the ankles of statues. There are times i lose this thread. Times laughing in the evening am by morning lost in tears.

*Schopenhauer is often cited as a fit subject for laughter, because he praised suicide while seated at a well-set table. The men lowered themselves into their places, gravely this time, not joking. In the right background, the Gudrun School (the Helen-Lange School of former years) blocking out the iron hodge-podge of the Schichau Dockyards as far as the big hammer crane. Thus began my closest childhood friendship which ripened into a romantic attachment. Since those happy days, the first four volumes have come out in the clear. "Your hands are 'wakan'; treat them as such!" Later, when Peter was in a state of breakdown and madness **he turned away and was repelled by me.** The press photograph is a message. This universal peace, following on the beating of the spears into pruning hooks or ploughshares, requires not just occasional chastity on the part of some, but a deep and committed chastity on the part of all - this to achieve a reconciliation between men and women that physical love, with its strong, cruel passion, makes impossible. The reason I don't get hung up with, well, say, integration, is that by the time Bob Newhart is integrated, I'm bigoted. The old poverty, Galbraith notes,*

64

*was general. The change seems to have been made while
the book was already being set in type (the title page of
the manuscript from which it was set is missing, indicating
perhaps that Nietzsche had taken it back to make the
alteration and that it was subsequently mislaid), and
this explains a few otherwise puzzling references to the
superseded title in the text. The will to truth, which is still
going to tempt us to many a hazardous enterprise; that
celebrated veracity of which all philosophers have hitherto
spoken with reverence: what questions this will to truth has
already set before us! Is not the greatness of this deed too
great for us? And even before having advanced very far in
this work, it seemed to me that the great break has to be
situated.*

Outside it is night. The streets are deserted. I'm shivering.
Not from cold. I need to cover four blocks uphill, two level,
five uphill. By the time I make it to the car park on the first
level I'm out of breath. Deserted. I walk through the narrow
alley out onto the church square. I cross the street and
pass my lawyer-friend's office. I walk the five blocks uphill
and knock on his door. It's dark. My stomach aches. I lean
against the wall. Door opens. His wife. Smiles at me, asks
me in. He gently pushes her aside. Closes the door after
him. Hits the side of my head with his open hand. Swears at
me to go away. I've run out of stuff. He doesn't care. You're
my lawyer-friend. I'll pay you back on Monday. I always get
money on Sundays. He puts his arm around my neck and
pulls me to him. Hits me. The side of his face is pushed up
against my head. I smell whiskey. I ask for a drink. Telling
me how dare I come round to his house. That we have an
arrangement. That he's going to fuck me up completely. That
he likes me but I've disappointed him. He tightens the grip
around my neck and using his knuckles rubs the top of my
head and then hits me hard. Car drives down the road. He
moves us swiftly across the porch against the wall where

no-one can see us. Wait here fuckhead. Goes inside. Leaves
the door open. I see narcs and security cops whose cocks
I suck for a hundred bucks a shot sitting on a couch inside
his lounge. They're passing round a crack pipe. Comes back.
Maybe the same day. Maybe I wait a year. Hands me a paper
packet three centimetres square. One-twenty on Monday. I'm
all smiles and ingratiating thanks. See him on Monday. He
can trust me. One-twenty on Monday. I walk down the mown
grass into the suburban night.

At home I put on nose plugs, and stick a diving snorkel in
my mouth. I open the packet carefully and empty it onto a
black ceramic tile. I remove the ink filament from a yellow
Bic pen. I use the larger opening to carefully divide the pile of
purple carbon into seven sections. I breathe deeply. Exhale.
Pull the nose plug off. Place the narrow opening of the pen
in my right nostril and the large opening over the seven piles.
Inhale. Deeply. Fall. Backwards. Inwards. Downwards. Fall.

is that kafka in new york city
or is this the post office
9th floor 1998
water dripping into buckets
dark corridors
plaster cracking off the walls
doors open onto empty rooms
people in flight on grassy islands
cacophony of time
fires break out spontaneously
wherever i look

Glass rains down on me. It's autumn here. I love you to
bits. All of your pieces. I swim in your golden shower.
An explosion. Everything's white. I can't move. Orgasm
involuntarily. Nausea. Voices. Someone shouts "The ammo
re-loads. We must move!" I hear more voices. A char woman
begins to vacuum the glass strewn across the carpet.

heat from the fire
blood from the heart
teeth from the mouth
salt from the ocean
gradient from the mountain
fire from the sun
buzz from the bees
colour from the rainbow
sand from the soil
pages from the book
mystery from wonder
certainty from pride

I can't see her. Another voice calls out. The walls give way to
the desert, the sea, sky. An abandoned fort rises above me.
Heat-waves distort my vision. Another explosion. I try to pull
the snorkel out of my mouth. My jaws have clamped shut.

#

Nietzsche said that truth is served when it is in a position
directly to procure salaries and advancement, or at least to
win the favour of those who have smack and honours to
distribute. My lawyer-friend is fucking me. He is standing
behind me. Has one arm around my neck. Magda, his wife,
is on her knees in front of me sucking my cock. His arm is
too tight around my neck. He keeps asking where his money
is. I can't speak. I am so in love. He keeps answering that
I did not bring it. This repetition is somehow directly tied to
the level of his arousal.

In manhood, where despair
turns to vengeance
destruction
sets in
place obscenity
w/a vengeance
of vengeance

coursing through
not only veins
and
headaches, but this
boyhood still
so low over
your dim
pummelling
eyes
behind me

His grip on my neck does not relent. He alternately pinches
my nipples and pulls my hair. He fucks me. He can't come.
Magda's a natural cock-sucker, but his monosyllabic fuck
cunt shit fuck gets me shoved to the floor, slapped hard.
Keep apologising. I move towards his cock, get slapped
again. Takes the condom off, pulls Magda down on him. I
get slapped a third time. Comes. Walks out. Magda follows. I
stare at the rows of leather-bound law reports. Comes back.
Says, so fuck off.

#

"I think though that it is important for me to tell you what
you probably don't need to be told and that is that friendships
are always compromised when money comes into the picture.
You have a habit of assuming that because you don't have
money and perceive everyone around you to have money that
they will automatically be responsible for you to some extent.
That is not fair and can freak people out. I don't want to go
into it too much because I know it is a subject that freaks
us both out but unless you examine this problem as small
and petty as it may be I am afraid that you are not going to
understand why things happen."

#

no one else would either. The Bandit's house had differed in no way from the common houses of the village. Seriousness of mind was a prerequisite for understanding Newtonian physics. The faces might sympathize, but I had been marked out for trouble. Vergil had to kick it the rest of the way. "Poor Carla," he said in Stuart's voice. A man like that would have money in his purse, and Howie would have bet a whole copper that his boots were new, too. In one corner was an overflowing bookcase, haphazard stacks of books and magazines stuffed into the shelves, piled on the floor beside it. + New edition. Yippie! "Dr. Harrow wants me to be certain you check your medications." From the way he leaned on the railing, the tilt of his head, and the easy way he appraised her, Caroline could dBase his whole history. He sat there for a moment, restlessly flexing his fingers like a synth musician whose solo performance had been aborted by a loose connector. "I'll interview him to determine whether he's in possession of contraband technology." **Water slid inside his boots,** *Holographic murals filled the walls, illustrating the life of the Compassionate One. As the morning passed, the sun moved away from the stained glass, and the room's interior went to gloom. Got a ripple in the Hemingway channel. Now, him I do know... but that's all I know. (The United Europe into which Malise was being initiated was, like any young state, economical with the truth.) Austen's eyes closed without his permission. In a rickshaw on thrones Level, Ceryl Waxwing watched a moujik girl die. I've told William, and he approves, or at least he does not tell me he objects. Anything that can alter plasm generation is supposed to be in the overlays or the updates. Sid was chipping away at a splash of grey concrete that marred the neat dark band. Maria Deluca had ridden past the stinking hole in Pyrmont Bridge Road for six days running, certain each time, as she'd approach'd, that she'd be greeted by the reassuring sight of a work team putting things right. "Instead of like Marilyn Monroe, "I said, looking* *around the room for Mayer. A Gray Line Tours bus pulled in from North Capitol.*

#

Fifth letter to Cherry:

Listen, thank you. It's an online conference so I can participate. Here's the abstract. Please let me know what you think?
xxx

Paper presented at the 8th Annual Qualitative Methods Conference: "Something for nothing"
1 May to 30 September 2002

Title: RADICAL CANT (even with excitement)

ABSTRACT:

"He closes your eyes
and he hands you a dream
you have your promise, your Midnight Promise"
— Jeffrey Lee Pierce

"I want to awaken the greatest mistrust of myself: I speak only of things I have experienced, and do not offer only events in the head."
— Friedrich Nietzsche

"It is not the height," says Zarathustra, "it is the abyss that is terrible." Contrary to popular belief, the abyss is not a place, it is a moment in perpetual motion, a moment of "darkness and consolation". The contradiction is intentional.

Torn between Superman and Mankind, between the heights and the abyss, Zarathustra must find a way of living with a permanently cracked "I", a permanently cracked subjectivity.

This has nothing to do with madness, and even less to do with Nietzsche.

Zarathustra seeks inner preconditions in place of practical conclusions. This is why there is no "theory" or "radical cant" of the eternal return (or of anything else) in Nietzsche's writings. He made no midnight promise, and didn't expect to receive one either.

Rather, he sought "a life" – a means of living which would enable practical conclusions to lie where inner preconditions determined they should fall. He sought to "live blindly among men, as if [he] did not recognise them".

Nietzsche was the first philosopher to mind his own business.

Zarathustra opposed Radical Cant with Manly Prudence:
"I let myself be deceived, so as not to be on guard against deceivers."
"I am more considerate to the vain than the proud."
"I do not let your timorousness spoil my pleasure at the sight of the wicked."
"I sit among you disguised, so that I may misunderstand you and myself."

Radical Cant is constitutive of the world and is entirely fictional.
Radical Cant seeks to unmask truth, revealing nakedness.
Radical Cant hates all masks and simulated surfaces.
Radical Cant interrogates the world as if it were a subjectivity.
As if it were an individual with a personality.
As if it were not unknowable and entirely fictional.
As if it were an object to be understood
As if it were a State to be achieved.

[No Full-Length Paper contained within manuscript]

#

Sixth letter to Cherry:

Hello glorious fucking laser beam, xxx fistings facials db's
da's and 20ways to you! But listen, some cunt taped fucking
gospel from radio pulpit over all my husker du cassettes.
Please use some of the cash from this next review and get
me all their stuff again. I'm sure its all available on CD now.
And your letter so rocked!!! Made me remember the first time
we met. This beautiful chick walking towards me all smiles
and great tits. I slapped your face and you slapped me right
back and my glasses ripped the top of my nose and then
crashed on the pavement. I'll never forget what you said after
you bandaged me up back at your place after you sucked me
off four times in a row. Do you remember Cherry? You said:
"why don't you just ask".
So anyway, I wrote you a poem. Just for you. It's called:
"pale dark pale blue laser sonic beam". Then I put my review
after that.

pale dark pale blue laser sonic beam

for cherry

electric rays. sonic beams. lasers
pale blue
dark blue   pale dark pale blue laser sonic beam
pale blue
the back of your skull the forehead of mine
linked. joined. cut through. severed. but joined.
pale dark pale blue laser sonic beam
the back of my skull. the forehead of yours.
laser sonic beam communication.
laser sonic beam join.
laser sonic beam same.
sameness. sameness. sameness.
I same. I same. You same.

sameness. sameness.
laser sonic beam. no difference.
pale dark pale blue.
pale dark pale blue.
pale pale pale blue.
pale pale blue
pale
blue. sea blue. broken dark blue. laser
bbbsssssssssssssssssss...... bsp.bssssssss.......
dark. pale dark pale blue overhead.
overhead laser sonic beam
forehead hole. blood
backhead hole. blood
congealing in hair.
glass dome. 180°
raw bleeding stump. winds in dome. howl. howl.
howls. dust
dust stings sand
howling
pale dark pale blue laser sonic beam
blue. sea blue. broken dark blue. laser
bbbsssssssssssssssssss...... bsp.bssssssss.......
pale dark pale blue laser sonic beam
I love you my pale dark pale blue laser sonic beam
pale dark pale blue laser sonic beam
--

Your black cock in Christ,
GOD (Getting Over Death)
xxx

and here's the review:

NIETZSCHE – Lou Salomé
University of Illinois Press, 2002

Friedrich Nietzsche fell into a state of mental and physical
paralysis in 1889. By that time he had written twelve

books, nine of which had been published. He did not write anything whilst in a state of madness. The final ten years of his existence were spent in mute paralysis. No philosopher has been more maligned than understood, more quoted than read.

Lou Salomé's book is unique. It attempts to present the "thought-experience" of Friedrich Nietzsche, the "confessions in his philosophy." For this it has been criticised, and neglected. It is interesting to note that Salomé published her book on Nietzsche in German, in 1894. It was translated into Danish in 1911, French in 1932, and Japanese in 1974. The book was first translated into English in 1988 in an expensive and hard to find hardcover edition. This is its first English appearance in affordable paperback.

Many years before, she actually discussed her idea of a book on him. Nietzsche responded enthusiastically: "your idea of reducing philosophical systems to the personal records of their originators is truly an idea arising from a 'brother-sister brain'. In Basel, I myself taught the history of ancient philosophy in just this sense..."

The critical magazine *Choice* felt that Salomé's book, "skirts the more technical aspects of his thought but faithfully presents his psychological observations and his poetic-mystical way of thinking and writing." This is not true. Editor and translator Siegfried Mandel, is no closer to the truth when he states that Salomé's "analytical" approach blunted the force of Nietzsche's "metaphorical and creatively iconoclastic" thinking.

Lou Salomé's book shows that there are three instances or moments of difficulty in reading Nietzsche. The first difficulty concerns his style. "I want to awaken the greatest mistrust of myself: I speak only of things I have experienced and do not offer only events in the head." And to convey this, he not only re-writes the book on philosophical discourse, but also on style. The aphoristic form, reaching perfection in two bewildering works – "Dawn" (1881), and "The Gay Science" (1882) – whilst not invented by Nietzsche was certainly perfected by him. According to Salomé, "The style of these works came about through the willing, enthusiastic, self-sacrificing, and lavish expenditure of great artistic talents ... and an attempt to render knowledge through individualised nuancing, reflective of the excitations of a soul in upheaval." As he wrote to Salomé in 1882 concerning the teaching of style: "Of prime necessity is life: a style should live."

The second difficulty concerns Nietzsche's use of masks. Navigating his masks is exhausting and can produce a feeling of falling through his texts (the text suddenly flipping into the opposite of its apparent sense). This can occur within the pages of a single work, or across the spectrum of his individual works.

"People who think deeply feel themselves to be comedians in their relationship with others because they first have to simulate a surface in order to be understood." These masks, or "simulated surfaces" occur throughout Nietzsche's work. According to Salomé: "That which Nietzsche seems to combat most strenuously, is what he fully incorporates into his theories, with extreme consequences and meanings..." And elsewhere, she notes that "Nietzsche takes up new ideas as he finds them, with a certain uncritical dependence. The new theories as such form only a temporary 'foreground philosophy'... while conflicts play themselves out decisively within the hidden inner background." Whilst these may appear to be contradictions, they are no such thing. They are instead, intensifications, the workings of self-overcoming: "Who has achieved his ideal, at the same time surpasses it..." Deep thinkers, according to Nietzsche, not only need and love masks, but "around every deep spirit there continually grows a mask."

This leads to the third and most intense difficulty in reading

Nietzsche: the idea of the eternal return - the core of his philosophy. According to Salomé, the first intimations of the idea of eternal return occur in 1882. Presented in an aphorism in "The Gay Science", the idea is masked, "hidden under the cloaks of light" - the kind of "prank Nietzsche revelled in", as Salomé has it. He also entertained ideas of grounding this idea in practical physics. But one must look more carefully here, because this first formulation of the eternal return, this foregrounded presentation, will be reversed later on.

Initially, as an hypothesis, the eternal return is an horrific, terrifying cycle: "...nothing new will be added; instead, every pain and every pleasure and every thought and sigh and everything inexpressibly small and great of your life must return to you, and all in the same series and sequence."

But because Salomé has small, beautiful ears, Ariadne's ears... she follows the profound change that occurs in this idea of eternal return. Firstly, Nietzsche gets sick. She is prescient in her observation: "falling ill because of thoughts and recuperating through thoughts" as it is during these years (1882-1885) that Nietzsche writes his magnum opus "Thus Spoke Zarathustra" (only published in 1892).

Zarathustra of course, reverses the thrust of the eternal return (as Nietzsche removes the idea of the return of the same, the idea of cycle) because these specific ideas were making him sick. As Salomé notes, "Instead of finding a scientific basis, Nietzsche's philosophy found an inner inspiration – his own personal inspiration." Salomé sees this new formulation of the eternal return as a "mystical revelation".

She then presents (or grows) something of her own mask, for in order to further articulate the eternal return, she presents a little foreground-philosophy-effect of her own, an insertion of an idea "hidden under the cloaks of light". She notes that for Nietzsche, suffering has value for the pursuit of knowledge, that he "did not wish to be saved from the pain of a teaching he feared, but [...] to become fruitful through it, to learn from it, and become its prophet..." And for these reasons, she continues, "the theoretical outlines of the recurrence ideas are never actually drawn with clear strokes; the outline remains pale and indistinct and retreats completely behind practical conclusions – the ethical and religious consequences – that Nietzsche seemingly derives from them, while in fact they serve as an inner precondition for him."

The "pale and indistinct" theoretical outlines of the eternal return, which hide behind the practical conclusions (which are ethical and religious consequences) are in fact not hiding at all. And this time, the "prank" is Salomé's – faithful reader (Ariadne!) that she is. Remember that Salomé set out to write a very specific book on Nietzsche, one which attempts to present the "thought-experience" of Friedrich Nietzsche, the "confessions in his philosophy".

Her text succeeds superbly, as it emulates Nietzsche, just as Nietzsche and his thinking-experiments were indistinct emulations of one another. In plain English – he lived his ideas as perhaps no other philosopher ever has, and that is the Nietzsche Salomé presents. He was not writing for an audience, and his thought-experiments were carried out on himself alone – "suffering has value for the pursuit of knowledge". Living his ideas so intensely, he had to create Zarathustra and a host of other figures and animals in order to represent his thought or to become his own prophet.

Salomé's book remains one of the rare instances of intelligent consideration given to Nietzsche's philosophy. The writer for *Choice* magazine makes a crucial (and very basic) error – you cannot separate "technical" from "psychological" aspects of Nietzsche's philosophy. Mandel similarly falls into error by reducing the complexity of Nietzsche's philosophy into "metaphorical and creatively iconoclastic" thinking.

It's not a matter of different types of thinking in Nietzsche, but the levels of intensity with which one "must want to experience the great problems with one's body and one's soul." This is the challenge of what has been described as Lou Salomé's "beautiful" book.

I dream a dream of freedom every night here in my cell. Since I dream the dream, I am the dream. I am free. I am at school and there's peals and shrieks of laughter, shouting, everyone's occupied in groups. I am alone on a sports field doing handstands and cartwheels, and raging from one end of the field to the other. Then I black out. Come to. All the other kids are staring at me. Fuck it. Who needs them. So I do flips to the other side of the field. Then I black out. I come to. The headmaster is walking towards me with his arms outstretched. He is an electric eel. He tells me he loves me. He says to come to his office with him. He says he's got something to show me, that I mustn't be afraid. So I follow him to the administration building. It is crowded with thousands of people. The corridors are a maze of dead ends, and circles. I get lost. I black out. Come to. Decide to weird this pasture for better shitholes yet. Fetch my bike in the shed. Tuck myself in to the bed I've constructed above my bike.

squeeze
my eyes tight
asleep
I swear
and way down
in my rickety fear of
losing you
the curtains
shut
the door
closed

I don't sleep
as it rains
I fear the
indulgence of your
fucking beating drowning
me to sleep
if I listen too hard
will you call my bluff
and stop?

I cycle furiously all along the railway track. Scrap metal
dealers line the tracks on the other side, and I wave hello. I
live in a house at the switching yard. But my bike's shaking
violently, and I'm having a hard time staying on it. Then it
collapses and the wheels roll off and fall onto the grass. I
get off the bed and try to put it all together again. I black
out. I come to. Fuck it, I'll ride the bed home instead. In
my room, my bed starts to shake and bounce off the floor. I
light a cigarette and try to forget about it. Tastes good. Then
I notice that my door has been open all along, so I get up to
close it. But it won't latch properly, and I'm scared of falling
out of my carriage as the train is rocking badly from side to
side. The bed starts up again and causes the carriage to lurch
dangerously. As it rights itself the door slams closed and the
latch holds this time. I become aware of what I had thought
was the screeching of brakes, but are now unmistakably
screams. So I open the door to let the screams out, and
the scenery becomes my room, and my room becomes the
scenery. Then I black out. I come to. Dad comes into my
room speaking Egyptian, which I don't understand. He is
saying that he's come to narrate my history. I'm sitting on a
bench in the city, he says, and I'm with this other guy. We
light up. It's Jean Baudrillard. Hello manno, he says. Fuckit,
I say. So we get up and walk through the deserted streets.
Take a short cut through the Carlton Centre. Walk up the
escalators. On the landing is a beautiful woman, luminescent
blue. She's lying in a pool of water, dressed in a ballerina's
tutu. It's Cherry, says Baudrillard. Yes, we've got to get

that train, I say. So we pick her up, and carry her back to
Baudrillard's place. Walking across the fields, I try to do flips
but I keep dropping Cherry, so I stop trying. An electric eel
slithers through the grass. Its needle teeth drip slime. The
other kids all stare at us.

The Black Steer is red neon on brick we walk under hoping
for a table all the while holding hands and telling you over
my third or fourth whiskey that I'd like to fuck you on the
table at last we order and wait another cigarette you're
beautiful sucking on your B'n'H my Gauloise feeling loaded
between my fingers smoking hot lemon water finally drives
your pale thighs from my mind and you collapsing beside me
my eyes lock onto your bra-strap beneath the white T-shirt
you've borrowed for the evening and I light another cigarette
on returning I watch to see if others watch too sitting
down you smile at me and yes no black bits of charcoal
between your teeth I leave (trailing your gaze the length of
the restaurant) stand at the urinal naphthalene fumes you
pay the impersonal price we split at the table before leaving
bridging the gap between two people resolutely separate with
entwined fingers driving you deal with the man asking for
money in darkness sticky with impending rain and decades-
old obsequious hatred these one-way sentences ending
in cul-de-sacs the rain your tears follow turns my heart to
embrace a darker night and a shirtless man shivering some
cold morning on an overnight bus in the middle of nowhere I
note the red depressions covering your naked body from the
clothes left on the bathroom floor the veranda's old wicker
armchair supports this view of the city our weight your joint
my cigarette and penetration's necessity your smoke's sweet
aroma blends exotically with my black tobacco and reclining
our obscenity can again abscond the immediate chasm our
sex serves to heighten this apartment channels hardening
layers of sentiment in heaps along the corridor my lamp casts
its light roundly on my squared writing pad illuminating our

excursion and your heaving mass seething this darkness we swim as a dream

#

"He's too old!" the boy said. Their managers all drive HumVees. "What became of the chems?" Maytera Mint managed to keep her voice steady. I looked at my watch. "Your tickler". The stage was white, horse-shoe shaped, backed by a giant Diacora depth-effect back-projection screen, a shimmering white curtain like an untouched canvas. Then all other so-called human triumphs, or moderate successes, products of anybody's reasoning processes and labours - and what are they, if higher than them all, more academic, austere, rigorous, exact are the methods and the processes of the astronomers? In 1929 André Malraux published his first novel, The Conquerors, *a story of the leaders of the Chinese Revolution of 1925. "Just sweep and clear and shaddup." I would almost go so far as to say that that is how things should be; in fact they never are. "As a matter of interest, Unkoo," says Zazie, "when you talk crap like that, do you do it on purpose or can't you help it?" They could be called love affairs, I suppose. "But, Mamma, you wouldn't go away - you wouldn't leave Papa and..." That's what they say. His very first piece of research was in his third year at the University, when he was deputed by the Professor of Comparative Anatomy* **to investigate a detail in the anatomy of the eel**, *which involved the dissection of some four hundred specimens. The source of our•findings does not seem to me to deprive them of their value. They spread far beyond the Australian totem races. Soon afterwards he entered the Physiological Laboratory under Brucke, and worked there happily for six years. Before very long Freud began to make changes both in the procedure and in the underlying theory; this led eventually to a breach with Breuer, and to the ultimate development by Freud of the whole system of ideas to which he soon gave the name of psycho-analysis.*

Certainly there was no softness in her of that kind of which Mrs. Stone had felt a need. In fact, I behaved very badly.

#

It's deathly silent in the city as the sound of my trousers rasps with each step I take and I take many. There is no-one about and the terror of the catastrophe deafens me with its silence. Then a light shines bright and brighter on the horizon, and a voice from the depths of silence roars in distortion you are today what you are tomorrow as I drive in the stakes as old as I am sweating all the liquid as old as I am there and I lose my self puts lips against their lips are cold and hard hand-shakes with hands of corpses reaching out to me are as dead as her charred body impales my world is consumed by her ecstasy rips my face to bleeding shreds are all that's left naked bleeding crying on your floor is as dirty as I am eaten alive by giant ants are gnawing my brain hurts when impaled by a charred body is always all that's left right left right left right left right into the arms depot is situated to the left right left right left right left of the granary was our favourite hiding place was the bum in the park said he loves me and I want to be with him I am not afraid of the dark he believes is in God is light information or opaque walls which encrust me with caresses are pincers of a scorpion pin me down with caresses are information to my brain is encrusted with caresses are pincers of a scorpion pin me down with caresses smother my eyes miss my watch glass cracks with the time of being fucked by the scorpions poisonous tale shoots up over its head has now got my eyes open to three witches throw scales into a plopping hot cauldron is propped up over a fire becomes foul breaths chanting joltingly hypnotic witches chanting witches warming up in hell are three and one to lose one self in to the cauldron go two screaming foetuses and the pumpingly manic suckings of the giant fly invoke only scorn from the witches one way or another you get only trouble follows those encrusted in opaque walls gonna getcha getcha getcha blondie

#

In the city, I meet a woman called Suicide tells of how she'd
like to be my plaything, of my mind and how she works it in
my daydream a million times before I seduce Suicide never
lies when she speaks of death and desire, tells you just how
just where just when, tells you a million times before you
seduce Suicide tells you when your mind will fragment, take
your pieces and rename them turning others inside out, tells
you she'd rather die alone than have you refuse her.

#

Dear Magda

Today is much like any other day, I stare you down, you shoot
right back, I occlude, I occlude.

Let words mean things! Let them stick! Let meaning
suffocate, allowing the extraction we move by. Here in my
little room, I have a line of laundry strung from door post to
window-frame, and a giant African-old Syringa tree deformed
and metonymising our memories. (that susurration? a
weeping God's abeyance, the cicatrices of time) – all of which
comes squarely back to laundry, wind, Syringas and you. xxx
Strangers knocking on my door, go away! You knock on my
tin shack, but I am in my mansion. You fill me with fear and
dread. No! No! Come in. Come in.

No matter.

I am a double agent.

"Sir, we are reduced to the common depidity, we grow
whiter everyday. We are aware of a growing luminosity, a
centeredness – Europe is crystalising under tectonic forces.
All becomes home."

Time: bastard. Crickets and Christmas beetles, beetles I've never met in this gentle light, soft breeze, the sun rises over you. The day has broken and will soon hit the thirty-degree barrier. Soon the beetles and the wilted shrubbery will know the interminable and intimate stitches of time.

But my gaze shifts to the sideway rushing by the car, then fills an entire valley of desire. I take you in, take you in my gaze, drink you, wrench you from yourself (or is that me?) This is nature's comeuppance: let the horses roam/let the sky be sea.

xxx

#

Comet ducked under the half lowered bars. **"You can have those too," she said.** *She held out a pen and a typed paper. Nothing was ever where he expected it to be. The woman was somewhere behind the house, cutting down the remains of a small rose pergola. The earth flowed around him like a warm, alluvial river. During the months before the divorce he had carefully observed the characteristic signs - the loss of weight and appetite, the cavalier neglect of both staff and clients at his architect's practice, his growing reluctance to go out of doors, the allergic skin rashes that sprang up if he stood for only a few seconds in the open sunlight. The fields had been covered with the dead bodies of gulls and magpies whose mouths were clogged with this silvering gum. In his mind World War III represents the final self-destruction and imbalance of an asymmetric world, the last suicidal spasm of the dextro-rotatory helix, DNA. Thinks I'm fixing to grab-ass, he thought as he snaked among the people. "As far as what you're wearing and all, you look just fine." "Birdie Ludd," she said, "sometimes you make me sick." "I'm, uh, adjusting it, Catz." I crawled under the waist-high lengths of thick black chains guarding the doorway, scuttling on all fours until I could sag into the worn colourless couch by* *the stereo. During his last week, in Professor Crossbow's house off the Tethys Reef, sixty miles from Telset, he edited them. Being awake in a lifeless body was not an entirely new experience for me. One Eye went rigid. The haunting "Tahiti in Terms of Squares" (1978), with its nonlinear suggestions of a new (or perhaps external) order of beings is all rush. After a few moments he put his tin plate down and sat staring dully to the south, out over the darkened lands beyond the river, just barely visible in the dim light of a crescent moon. Eighty thousand dollars for a corner lot on Calumet Avenue? A part of him knew that the arc of his self-destruction was glaringly obvious to his customers, who grew steadily fewer, but that same part of him basked in the knowledge that it was only a matter of time. VIDEO: CLOSE-UP of SCHUYLER, his eyes still open*

#

Dear Magda

Well, the night is my friend, I hope it never leaves me. You punned again this morning (in my dream). The flat was cold and silent, idsturbing, you said. And now I fear addressing you, case I riddle your body with words.

I woke up and realised I'd missed the stop, I was asleep, I missed my stop – now I don't know where I am. Woke up within Paulus Nomad and realised I went to sleep at some point before but can't determine when exactly – now everything's changed. Like a burlesque dancer on "Show Girls", Myrna, "I just feel so lost"

the line
connection
holding
engagement
sounds of the ocean
causes without effect

a relation essential invaluable
"at once / the tease / of possibility" – (holgar czukay)
stranger to myself and
stranger still to others
a surfer gliding
timing the closing roll of danger
crashing at his heels

--

time for me to go
don't know where to
don't know if i'll leave here to go there
don't know if there is here or where there is
don't know where i'll stop if i'll know when i stop
don't know if i'll stop when i'm still going or stop when i stop
don't know if stop and go
will still have any meaning
when i'm going

--

\#

Dear Sir Co.

Gratuleted you Mr Wessels in The name of God I am
Physically Emotionally and Spiritually fit under the
Circumstances of this Place Deathrow Hopping That you
are also in the same Physical Condition I Hope you'll Enjoy
Reading This letter in Such a way That you Imagine, my
Presence Mr Paul Wessels Well Sir I Hope God Bless you
When I Say God Bless you I mean God Help you and love
you Hold his light To Shine Above you, Well Sir. God Suffers
With His Peoples, Hold on Tight To God Sir God Can Change
Things Well Mr Wessels Take your Responsibilities Seriously
A message of Hope Well Mr Wessels I Decide To Wrote you
This letter As. A. Clamency to you Well Sir I am Willing

To Address you my Reasons Well Sir life is full of lovely
Surprises Not a day Passes but What Some beautiful Though
often Small Experience Breaks Through life's monotony
and reminds you That God Is Good and loves me It is The
Acknowledgement And Appreciation of The unexpected
Surprises That Enriches life beyond All Expectation and
enables me To Thank God for his Wonderful Goodness Well
Sir Make a Practice of daily looking for The hidden loveliness
of life Granted There are Plenty of things That are hurtful
and ugly and They Seem To Swamp most of What is healthy
an beautiful It is So easy To dwell upon The Negative aspect
of life and lose Sight of The Positive and of infinite Value
The beautiful Surprises of life are Present for All Who are
Prepared To See and appreciate them iT has been Wisely
Said That beauty is in The eyes of The beholder. How True
you may have become So familiar with your life Style That
you Cannot imagine That iT Could Contain Any Surprises or
Possess Any beauty but iT is Possible To Discipline you Sir,
Well Mr Wessels I am Willing To Entrue my Self Well Mr
Wessels I am From Port Elizabeth I Was Sentence To Death
This year Well Sir What I Want is That I Want you Sir To do
me a Clamency By The Acting State President Mr FW De
Klerk So Mr Wessels I Hope you'll Agree This Point Please
Well Sir my Case is Going To be Argu in Bloemfontein After
September but now I Don't Now What Date Mr Paul I Was
Sentence This year On This Date 89.03.6 Well Mr Paulus
My God Jesus Christ He Told me in My Dream you are The
One Who Can Help me and my Advocate Mr xxxxxxx He is
From Grahamstown I Would Be Very Glad if you Can Contact
Him He Would Gives you more Information About The Case
you Can Find Him by This Telefoone Telephone Number
Sir Mr xxx xxxxxx Tel xxxxx St Georges Chambers 108
High Street Grahamstown Well Sir I do belive you Will Also
Encarrege your View Point because I now you are a Christian
for The Sake of love of Christians And To Love each Unother
between Black And White for The Reason Peace Nagotiation
in our Beloved Country Because We All From This Country
Well All Of Us We have Birth From This Country We Must

Try Bouth To bring Peace We must Not Allow our Country
To be DismaTle by Pressure for The Sake of Future of our
Country To Bring A Very Very Good Salution To under Stand
each unother To Avoid Circumstances Reasons Because Sir
Our mighty Father in heaven We Bouth Nation do Love Us
All The Same Why We do not Want To Corresponde Each
unother The Time Ripped To be We must Bouth Nations
Black & White Show A Very Strong Progress for Tomorrow
Well Mr Wessels That's the end of my Spelling I Hopes God
Bless you And you Familly Have A God Tim And Good Time I
Hope you Will Answer me Sir As Soon you Receive This letter
And Fewlines I Would Very Proud And Glad In My Spiritually
in Christ I Bless All Studants There In Rhodes Studants of our
Country And Other Countrys

From your Faithful Black Brother in Christ

Dear Magda

This is the end. Train rolls out the station. I'm left with your
image like a scalp dripping blood from my hand.
The runway slopes in buckled sections separated by ruptures
of snapped concrete. We shuffle like mutants, sick, and
knowing the sea of you is spelt with the "c" of cunt. The I is
lost in the c of you. We look the same, I look the same. I'm
lost in a sea of you. All of you. This is the end, my offence,
my word-bomb, disturbing the populace. My poem starts with
everything and ends in nothing. I need some sort of skin. I'm
all out of my own.

The sun's slid off this canvas, the yolk is ruptured. Ducking
and weaving, bullets zip past my head. Sea Gulls! Falling
shards of Heaven with their terrible screams. An ocean's acid
rolling onto this beach of crushed glass.

whales beach

    birds plummet

        earthwards

Hand in hand we walk to the water's edge. Black water-hyacinth gives the appearance of a carpeted hallway as we slowly make our way in.

All things being everywhere, nothing is equal - this is not a pretty poem. I harbour deep semantic drives at night I dream of writing bodies out their pain or trying to relieve myself I run my eyes on through their words to exit this dark consciousness, this page of mortal suffering no less real for having been written.

The vomit of poetry: who returns, recoils. Who recoils, returns to echolalia, the saddest word in the world. Still, this ache of release, the only violence is relief's explosion.

You're an abyss I'm written into Magda, an abyss I'm writing into.

        #

end
poem
offence

        word-bomb
     disturbing the populace
        everything

                nothing
                  skin
                  out

#

Judge: "Please sit down."

Paulus Nomad: "I won't sit down."

Judge: "Then I must draw the following points to your attention. We now intend to proceed to the examination of personal data."

Paulus Nomad: "That doesn't interest me."

Judge: "At this point you have an opportunity to give your own account of yourself. The consequence of your failing to do so will be that we must proceed with the trial."

Paulus Nomad: "All I have to tell you is that I've been dragged in here by force. In the circumstances I'm not giving an account of myself. I'm going down again now, and naturally you'll continue with this spectacle."

Judge: "It is your duty as a defendant, to remain here."

Paulus Nomad: "If you won't expel me from court anyway, I'll climb out over this balustrade somehow."

[Makes to leave the dock, but is stopped by the guards.]

Judge: "Please sit down, Frau Paulus Nomad."

Paulus Nomad: "I have no intention of sitting down."

Judge: "You have no intention of sitting down. Would you at least make use of the microphone, so that we can hear what you have to say?"

Paulus Nomad: "I don't want anything to do with this. I'm in no position to defend myself, and naturally I can't be defended either."

Judge: "Will you give an account of your personal details?"

Paulus Nomad: "In these circumstances, I will not give any account of my personal details."

[Makes to leave the dock, but is stopped by the guards.]

Paulus Nomad: "I want to go."

Judge: "It is your duty, as a defendant, to remain here."

Paulus Nomad: "I'm not letting anyone force me, you arsehole!"

Judge: "Frau Paulus Nomad, I observe that you have just addressed me as 'arsehole', as 'you arsehole'."

Paulus Nomad: "Perhaps you'll take note of that. Get on with it and expel me, will you?"

Judge: "Paulus Nomad this is not a question of your own wishes."
Paulus Nomad: "Then list all the disturbances, or do I have to call you names? I'm finding this very difficult. You want to force me to stay here?"

Judge: "It's not that I want to; I must."

Paulus Nomad: "What are you waiting for, do you want to provoke abuse or what?"

Judge: "I don't want to provoke anything, I would far rather you refrained from abuse."

Paulus Nomad: "I shall disrupt the trial, this manoeuvring of yours is a dirty trick."

Judge: "There is no dirty trick involved. The rules of procedure oblige me to act as I do."

Paulus Nomad: "So what do you want? Are you set on having physical violence, or what?

Judge: "I want you to sit down and take part in the hearing in an orderly manner."

Paulus Nomad: "Hell, it's filthy manipulation, the way you're forcing me to spend five minutes insisting you expel me. I simply want to be out of here."

Judge: "It is not a question of your personal wishes. Your duty as a defendant is to remain here."

Paulus Nomad: "Oh, allright, carry on with your ridiculous procedure. I shall create a disturbance."

Judge: "So far you are creating no disturbance."

Paulus Nomad: "Well, let me tell you, judge, you'd better expel me now or I'll find myself forced to abuse you."
Judge: "Herr Paulus Nomad."

Paulus Nomad: "Are you set on hearing it then? Alright, you can have it, you can have it all sorts of ways."

Judge: "I do not wish to hear it."

Paulus Nomad: "Well, you can hear me tell you you're a fascist arsehole."

Judge: "Ah, a 'Fascist arsehole'."

Paulus Nomad: "Now will you expel me?"

Paulus Nomad: "And me too, you old swine."

Paulus Nomad: "I'll say it again, judge, loud and clear; you're an old Fascist arsehole!"

Paulus Nomad: "We're not fit to stand trial, and owing to that we won't participate in this, you old swine."

Judge: "You have created a disturbance! You have planted word-bombs! I understood you to call me an old swine; did I hear that correctly or was I mistaken? I would like to have that ascertained; is it right? And you have called me a 'Fascist arsehole'."

#

Oh Mother Christ
every time i think of you
i want the love of a fascist woman
recognise me for being on the border
(slap)
it's raining every time i think of you
(slap)
under the radar always writing
Cherry on the back seat
Rodriquez on tape
Port Elizabeth,
Elizabeth Sun Hotel, 7:45 am
face the blue sky with these new boots so cyber-noir
gauloises smoking
feeling loaded
between my tears
stripping off this face

it's raining
every time
i think of you
it's raining

horror head
falling free
mission from god
today is not the day
coast is clear
the colour hurts
frozen
zoo
clipped
die like a dog
galaxy
cherry

every time, Mother Christ, every time
with your opalescent thighs, your hands
between your legs, this terrible rubbing out of my mind
with your sobs and groans shrieking fucking clatter while
trying to read Sacher-Masoch: "There is a painful stimulus in
the unfaithfulness of a beloved woman. It is the highest kind
of ecstacy."

every time
every
fucking
time I lose a piece of me in every cigarette
in every pair of cyber boots, plastic, so cyber-noir,
Port Elizabeth, Elizabeth Sun Hotel, 7:45 am
and she'll come back, she's to meet me here,
collect the bag
leave my face on the bus
you never came

i think of you, Mother Christ, rising from black waters
my eviscerated guts lying beside me
my oesophagus pumping oil as it spurts in a jerry can
dogdogs are shoving their snouts into my cavity ripping at my
lungs

Oh Mother Christ my hair rips out in chunks of bloodless skin
release me redeem me fuck me eat me
I feel your heat Mother Christ,

now –

i think of you

and its raining Mother Christ, your mouth salty sweet
cigarettes junk food (wimpy burgers) sex, panic, as i see you
now every time i think of you its raining greyhound overnight
to Joburg woman in the car we overtake hikes up her skirt
hide between her thighs and suck and suck and suck its
raining every time i think of you

every
every time i think of you

its raining

only shallow
loomer
touched
to here knows when
when you sleep
I only said
come in alone
sometimes
blow a wish
what you want
soon

"keep on," Mother Christ you sang, "keep on keeping me
from harm"

Grahamstown 1987, 1989 - Cape Town 2001, 2003

page 15: John Donne – Death Be Not Proud
from: Norton Anthology of Poetry, 1983 edition.

page 15: JM Coetzee – "I create myself ... I cannot stop now."
page 16: JM Coetzee – "My eye falls ... does not fulfill."
page 17: Alexander Kojève – "[H]umanity 'comes to light' ... such a desire."
page 17: Alexander Kojève – "For one ... Master's Slave."
page 18: GWF Hegel – "But the slave's consciousness ... his autonomy."
page 18: JM Coetzee – "The You has little ... cannot be reciprocal."
from: Dovey, Teresa. *The Novels of JM Coetzee*. AD Donker, 1988.

page 29: Sinclair Beiles – "and she brought a little boy for me..."
from: Doherty, Christo, Ed. *Porno Literature*. Bobbejaan Pers, 1989.

page 41: David Thomas – "use of a dog"
("Who would question the worth of a dog
Who would query the use of a dog?")
from: *Song of The Bailing Man*, Pere Ubu (1982).

page 47: Andrea Dworkin – "I am never real in his other descriptions of my
behaviour ... recognition is death." Dworkin uses the third person "She is
never real..." on page 22.
from: Dworkin, Andrea. *Intercourse*. Arrow Books, 1987.

page 61 : Meiling Jin – "We arrived ... in a lily white landscape..."
page 62 : Meiling Jin – "One day I learnt ... to chaos."
from: *Strangers in a Hostile Landscape* by Meiling Jin, cited by Homi K.
Bhabha in Appignanesi, Lisa, Ed. ICA Documents 6: Identity, 1987.

page 61 : Blondie – "one way or another"
from: *Parallel Lines* (1978)
cited in Kathy Acker's *Algeria*. Aloes Books, 1984.

page 85 : "Dear Sir Co." – found letter.

page 89 : Judge – transcript of Baader Meinhof trial.
from: Vague, Tom. *Televisionaries: The Red Army Faction Story
1963 – 1993*, (AK Press, 1994).

horror head, falling free, mission from god, today is not the day
coast is clear, the colour hurts, frozen, zoo
clipped, die like a dog, galaxy, cherry
Track Listings *from*:
Horror Head, Frozen, and Cherry EPs respectively. Curve.

only shallow, loomer, touched, to here knows when, when you sleep, I only
said, come in alone, sometimes, blow a wish, what you want, soon
Track Listing *from*:
Loveless by My Bloody Valentine. Creation Records. 1991.